"Don't talk such childish rubbish!"

At his harsh command, Cassandra turned her face away in humiliation. She had just told Saul that she loved him, and his words were like a whiplash on her spirit.

Relentlessly he went on. "You'll find your missionary lover when all this is over. You'll marry him, wear fancy bonnets and teach 'poor heathen children' that cats in England sit on mats. That's what you came to Africa for. Please spare me your absurd flights of fancy!"

But what Cassandra didn't realize was how much Saul hated to utter those brutish words. ..

Christina Laffeaty

is also the author of
Masquerade #56

Count Antonov's Heir

Princess Vezenski had asked Caroline to
be a bridesmaid at her wedding. But
how could Caroline go through with it?
For the princess was marrying Count
Antonov, the man Caroline loved deeply
and passionately.

Princess Vezenski had said it was
permissible in the rigid Russian aristocracy
to shed tears at a wedding. But Caroline
feared she would spill something far more
shattering than tears—for when her heart
broke, it might release its terrible secret...

...a secret that would surely plunge her
beloved Count Antonov into poverty
and humiliation.

Zulu Sunset

CHRISTINA LAFFEATY

A MASQUERADE FROM

W☉RLDWIDE

TORONTO · LONDON · NEW YORK

Masquerade edition published April 1981
ISBN-0-373-30063-8

Originally published in 1980
by Mills & Boon Limited

Printed in Canada

CHAPTER
ONE

CASSANDRA had dressed with particular care before stepping ashore at D'Urban, the seaport settlement of the British colony of Natal, for she had been unable to repress the foolish hope that Martin might be at the harbour to meet her. Of course he hadn't been there, and now, as she boarded the hired hackney cab with her maid Bridget, she wondered whether her clothes were not, perhaps, too modish and up to the minute for this outpost of the Empire.

Her gown, with its skirt kilted from the waist and its panniers which emphasised her slim hips, was the very latest style from Paris, and stamped her immediately as a fashionable young lady of substance. In lichen-green Indian cashmere, trimmed with velvet, it was matched by a mantelet which fitted tightly at her waist.

To complete the costume, her bonnet was of coarse white straw, lined with fluted muslin and trimmed with corded silk. Under the brim and around the crown alternate bouquets of pink and white hyacinths and green mosses flattered her pale complexion, her red-gold hair and her eyes which always changed colour according to her surroundings or her moods. At the moment they reflected the blue-green of the Indian Ocean which lapped D'Urban.

Had she made a mistake in ordering her wardrobe from Paris? she wondered uneasily. Would Martin think her frivolous and self-indulgent? But she had so much wanted him to see her in pretty things; the last time he had laid eyes on her she had been a clumsy, lanky girl of sixteen. Having adored him since child-hood, it was natural that she had wanted him to see that she no longer bore any resemblance to the plain child he had bade farewell in London, five years ago.

Martin was her second cousin, six years her senior. Tall, handsome, with clear-cut features and golden hair, he had always seemed to her the epitome of man-hood. When he had announced his intention of be-coming a missionary in remote Zululand, Cassandra had been stricken with grief, but his choice of vocation had also stirred her imagination and added a new idealistic dimension to the feeling she had for him. She had been striving consciously ever since to mould her-self into the kind of young woman of whom he would approve.

A few months ago, when she came of age and gained control of her inheritance, Martin had written her a letter of congratulation and had suggested, with ironic humour, that she might sweep crumbs from her over-laden table and make a donation to his mission. So much was needed; a hospital, a school for the children, a proper church in which to worship. Cassandra had been about to send him a draft for a generous sum when a sudden female ingenuity had shown her a way of forcing Martin to see that she had grown up, and was worthy of consideration as his bride.

There had been no one in London to gainsay her. Both her parents were dead, and the elderly relative with whom she lived was not greatly interested in her affairs. So Cassandra had written to Martin, indicating that she wished to come in person and see for herself how her money could best be spent.

To her surprise and delight, he had welcomed the suggestion at once, and had given her detailed instruc-tions on how to reach Zululand. It was unlikely that he would be able to leave the mission in order to meet her at the harbour, but she would have no difficulty in travelling to the interior if she did as he directed...

Her gaze went to the horizon. Somewhere beyond those distant hills, their crests opaque and glassy in the tropical sunlight, lay her destination.

The hackney had stopped outside the military head-quarters. Cassandra gathered her skirts, and allowed the driver to help her down. Telling Bridget that she would not be long, Cassandra approached a doorway at which two armed soldiers were standing guard.

'I have a letter of introduction to Colonel Thesiger,' Cassandra explained.

A few minutes later a young officer, Captain Bradley, was escorting Cassandra into the military commander's study. She could not help but be aware that Captain Bradley was casting admiring glances at her, and again she felt uneasy about her fashionable clothes.

Colonel Thesiger was an austere, aristocratic-looking man of middle age. He greeted Cassandra with punc-tilious courtesy, and invited her to sit down while he read the letter of introduction. He placed the letter on the desk afterwards. 'And how may I serve you, Miss Hudson?'

'My cousin, Martin Coleman, instructed me to ask you for an escort of soldiers to his mission in Zululand, sir.'

The Colonel and Captain Bradley exchanged glances. Then Thesiger said, 'I am afraid that is out of the question, Miss Hudson.'

Cassandra frowned. 'But my cousin assured me that it was quite a normal procedure——'

'In normal times, yes. But these are not normal times.'

'I don't follow, Colonel.'

'I shall try to explain, as briefly as possible. The Zulus have been overstepping the mark. Sir Bartle

Frere, the High Commissioner, has issued an
ultimatum to the Zulu king. If the terms of the
ultimatum are not met, our army will invade Zululand.'

Cassandra stared at him in alarm. 'You mean there is
to be a war?'

Colonel Thesiger allowed himself a smile. 'One could
scarcely call it a war, Miss Hudson, considering the
superiority of the British army over undisciplined tribal
savages. But it is true that there will be some skirmishes before the Zulus are brought to their knees.
Cetewayo, the so-called King, is an ignorant savage, a
murderous tyrant who must be taught his place.'

Cassandra twisted her hands together. 'My cousin
made no mention of any quarrel with Zululand, when
he last wrote to me! Has he been warned of the situation?'

The Colonel shrugged. 'All the missionaries were
informed of the developments. If they choose to ignore
the situation, that is their responsibility.'

'I am not in the least surprised that my cousin refused
to leave his mission. He is far too dedicated.' A dismay-
ing thought struck Cassandra, and she jumped up in
agitation. 'But Martin would never have exposed *me* to
danger! He was expecting me to arrive today, by the
Harlech Castle, and to request a military escort into
Zululand. If you are right, and he truly knows how
matters stand, he would have sent a message to me,
advising me what to do!'

Colonel Thesiger shrugged again. 'Perhaps he did
send such a message. Nothing seems more likely. But
communications between Natal and Zululand have not
been reliable lately. In the absence of any advice from
your cousin, you had best be guided by me, Miss Hudson. Remain in D'Urban until Zululand is no longer an
independent state ruled by savages. Where are you
putting up, by the way?'

'I had not given the matter any thought. I came directly here from the harbour—'

'I can recommend the Carlton,' Colonel Thesiger said briefly. 'It is a respectable and comfortable hostelry. Captain Bradley will escort you to your cab, and give the driver his instructions.'

The Colonel rose, signalling that the interview was at an end. Captain Bradley took Cassandra's elbow and steered her from the room. Once they were out of earshot, he said reassuringly,

'Don't be anxious about your cousin, Miss Hudson. The Colonel saw it as his duty to emphasise the dangers, but truly they are slight. The Zulus would not dare to worsen matters for themselves by harming a missionary, or any other British citizen, before the deadline of the ultimatum expires; by the time it does, everything will be over very quickly, and the Zulus subdued.'

Cassandra searched his face. 'But if there is so little danger,' she asked, 'why can't I be given an escort into Zululand?'

'For several reasons. The British army is to make an impressive show of massing on the frontier with Zululand, and all our troops are in training. Besides, it would be a diplomatic error for any of our men to enter Zululand under arms at the present moment. At the best they could be accused of exacerbating the situation; at worst they could be regarded as spies.'

Cassandra caught her lower lip between her teeth. 'Captain, if I followed Colonel Thesiger's advice, how long could I be expected to kick my heels in D'Urban?'

'Some months, I would say. Once the Zulus have been crushed there will be a mass of red tape to be cleared up before normality can be imposed.'

'*Months*!' Cassandra echoed, staring about her at the

brash new buildings of D'Urban, at the wide dusty road which was the seaport's main thoroughfare. What could one find to do here for months? And besides, she had set her heart upon being reunited with Martin by Christmas.

'Do you believe,' she addressed the captain again, 'that it would be quite safe for me to make the journey into Zululand at present, provided I could procure a reliable and independent escort?'

'Yes, I would certainly say so, Miss Hudson. The deadline for King Cetewayo to agree to the ultimatum falls in the New Year—the tenth of January, 1879, to be precise. It is now the fifteenth of December. That would give you ample time to reach the mission before a skirmish or two on the frontier decide the fate of Zululand for good and all.'

Cassandra nodded slowly. 'Very well, Captain. I shall go to the Carlton now, as Colonel Thesiger suggested, and make all haste to find an escort into Zululand.'

Captain Bradley hesitated for a moment. 'Miss Hudson, please don't quote me, but as fate will have it there is the very man putting up at the Carlton at present who would make the ideal escort for you. I would not have made the suggestion, otherwise, that you should go to Zululand against Colonel Thesiger's advice.'

'Who is this man, Captain Bradley?' Cassandra asked eagerly.

'They call him the Blue-Eyed Induna. An Induna is a Zulu chief. But this particular chief is a white man, of British parentage.'

'How extraordinary!' Cassandra exclaimed.

'Indeed. His name is Saul Parnell, and his history *is* extraordinary. It seems that his parents, border farmers, were killed by the Zulus during a raid, and he himself was taken as a small boy to live in the royal Zulu *kraal*, or village. One would think that he would nurse a grudge against the people who had murdered his parents, but instead he embraced the Zulu ways, and today he is a favourite with King Cetewayo and the Royal Family, and is ruler in his own right over some three thousand savages.'

'What a strange story,' Cassandra said, wide-eyed.

'Yes. As I said, he is putting up at the Carlton at present. He had come from Zululand with a request from Cetewayo for more time to consider the ultimatum; the request has been refused, and Saul Parnell is returning to his *kraal* tomorrow. Your cousin's mission station is no considerable distance out of his way. Ask the Blue-Eyed Induna to lend you escort.'

'I shall!' Cassandra nodded, her own eyes shining. 'Thank you, Captain!'

In the hackney cab, the driver—a young man of Liverpudlian origin—had obviously been whiling away the time attempting to flirt with Bridget. The little maid's freckled face was flushed, almost matching her carroty hair.

When Cassandra had to decide upon a maid to accompany her to Zululand, the choice had virtually been made for her. None of the older servants wished to venture into such a far-away, heathen land. But Bridget, only two years older than Cassandra herself, shy, quiet and alone in the world, had surprised her by volunteering for the post. So far she had embraced every new experience with the same stolid fortitude.

Briefly, Cassandra explained the situation to her, adding, 'I am sure there is no danger of our being affected by any fighting, but if you are afraid, Bridget——'

'Sure, I am not afraid at all,' the maid declared in her soft brogue. 'When do we leave, Miss Cassandra?'

'As soon as I have come to an arrangement with Mr Parnell. When we arrive at the Carlton I shall ask,

straight away, to be presented to him.' She frowned
doubtfully. 'Or should I change my costume first,
Bridget? What should one wear when meeting a white
Zulu Chief?'

'I daresay he will be wearing animal skins himself,
Miss Cassandra,' Bridget answered prosaically. 'And
your bonnet will seem very grand to him indeed. Why,
'tis plain that even the fashionable ladies of D'Urban
have never set eyes upon the likes of it before. Have you
not seen them staring? I'm sure such a poor half-savage
will be quite stricken dumb by your presence.'

Cassandra laughed, but she had to concede that her
bonnet *was* causing a small sensation among the ladies
they passed in their hackney. Perhaps, after all, it
would be more than suitable for the presence of a white
Zulu Chief.

The Carlton was a new building in baroque style,
deep-carpeted and comfortable. Its large reception
room was divided into intimate niches and cubicles by
the use of ornate pillars and decorative wrought-iron
screens. As soon as Cassandra had been assured that
adjoining bedrooms were available for herself and
Bridget, she left her maid to supervise the unloading of
their luggage and asked the reception clerk if an audience could be arranged with Mr Saul Parnell.

'Certainly, Miss Hudson,' he assured her. 'Please
follow me.'

Wondering a little at the lack of ceremony, Cassandra
set off after him as he led the way towards one of the
cubicles in the reception room.

'Mr Parnell,' she heard the clerk say, 'please allow me
to present Miss Hudson.'

The Blue-Eyed Induna had risen courteously to his
feet. Cassandra stared at him in mute astonishment.
This was no half-savage, such as she had been imagining. Far from wearing animal skins, as Bridget had

forecast, his clothes were casually elegant and lent distinction to his tall, well-built frame.

His physical appearance provided a shock, too. The penetrating, intensely blue eyes she had been expecting, of course; what she had not expected was that they were intelligent and somewhat cynical, set beneath heavy, arched dark brows. His hair was dark too, growing in a wing across his high forehead. His nose was straight, the set of his mouth firm. There was something implacable about his square jaw. But the biggest surprise was that he was young; no more than twenty-eight or twenty-nine years old.

'Please sit down, Miss Hudson,' he invited after the reception clerk had withdrawn. For a man who had been brought up with savages, his speech was remarkably cultured.

Cassandra took the proffered chair and wondered how to begin. 'I arrived in D'Urban this morning,' she said at last, 'on board the *Harlech Castle*——'

'Indeed.' His voice was polite and noncommittal.

'Yes. I——The thing is, Mr Parnell, I am bound for the Magwana Mission Station in Zululand, and I would be grateful for your escort on the way.'

'I see.' This time there was no politeness in his voice. It was hard, and held an unaccountable note of discouragement.

'Yes. My cousin, Martin Coleman, is in charge of the Magwana Mission.'

'I know him,' the Blue-Eyed Induna said without warmth.

'Oh . . .' Cassandra floundered. 'Well, I am joining him——'

'As a missionary, Miss Hudson?'

Something in his voice brought a flush to her cheeks. 'No,' she forced herself to say with dignity. 'Unfortunately I lack the dedication to aspire to that calling. I

want to help the mission in some financial way which
would do the most good. And I also hope to stay at least
for a while, and perhaps teach the little heathen children to read and write.'

She realised, by his expression, that she had somehow
said the wrong thing. One dark, arched eyebrow shot
up. 'In that bonnet, Miss Hudson?'

She flushed, and fingered one of the bouquets of
hyacinths inside the brim. 'Well, why not?' she
returned defiantly. 'Why should the little heathen children not have the chance to admire a pretty Parisian
bonnet?'

He stood up, his arms folded across his chest. 'Miss
Hudson,' he said tersely, 'you are as overweening in
your arrogance, as patronising and as ignorant as every
other do-gooder who has cursed Zululand with their
presence in the past. I will have no part in escorting you
to my country, to do your worst. Good day.'

He sketched a bow in her direction, and strode away,
leaving her standing there, bewildered and angry. Then
dismay swept aside all other feelings as she realised that,
without his escort, she stood little chance of reaching
Zululand. For a moment she toyed with the notion of
setting off after him, and begging him to reconsider.
But instinct told her that that implacable man was not
given to reconsidering any decision he had made.

She was still standing there irresolutely when,
around the corner of a pillar which separated the cubicle
from the next, a plump face appeared, wearing a benign
but apologetic expression.

'Dear child,' the owner of the face said, 'we could not
help but overhear your conversation. May we join you?'

'By all means,' Cassandra said automatically.

The plump face belonged to an equally plump body,
encased in a frock coat. He was of middle age, and
introduced himself as Daniel West, preacher.

'Call me Brother Daniel,' he invited. 'We of the Revived Apostle Movement look upon everyone as our brothers and sisters. This is Brother Alan, who shares my calling.'

Brother Alan was young and fresh-faced, with high curved brows which lent his expression a look of startled innocence. Cassandra shook hands with them somewhat bemusedly, and introduced herself.

They sat down, and Brother Daniel folded his hands earnestly in front of him. 'Miss Hudson—or may I call you Sister Cassandra?—I can perceive the hand of the Lord in your predicament. It was surely thus ordained. For, do you see, we can help one another!'

'I don't quite understand,' Cassandra said, blinking.

Brother Daniel fumbled in the pocket of his frock coat for a scrap of paper. 'A pencil, Brother Alan!' Swiftly, he began to sketch. 'See, Sister Cassandra, this is Zululand. This cross marks the spot of your cousin's mission station, Magwana. And just *here*, a little to the east, is the mission where Brother Alan and I are to carry out the Lord's work.'

'Oh, I understand now!' Cassandra's face cleared. 'You are travelling to Zululand too, to take up missionary work, and can escort me to Magwana! But that is wonderful!'

Brother Daniel gave a deprecating cough. 'Indeed, but there is one small obstacle to overcome. You see, Sister Cassandra, Brother Alan and I have been waiting for weeks now for funds to reach us from the Tabernacle in London. We had hoped that today, among the mail brought in by the *Harlech Castle*.... But alas, it was not to be. And the next vessel to arrive from England is not scheduled for another six weeks. And in the meantime our meagre funds are dwindling away in paying for our lodging here at the Carlton.'

He coughed again, in embarrassment. '"Ask, and

ye shall be given," the Good Book says. So I will pocket my pride, Sister Cassandra. If you could provide the funds to equip our expedition, Brother Alan and I will guide you into the interior and give you our protection.'

Cassandra gazed thoughtfully at him 'What would you need?'

'A wagon, a span of oxen, and provision. Oh, and horses. We shall need two hacks.'

'Why horses, if we are to travel by ox-wagon?'

'The Tugela River,' Brother Daniel explained, 'which forms the border between Natal and Zululand, is very deep and wide in places. It will be necessary to ferry ourselves and the provisions across on horseback, and persuade the oxen to swim to the other side, pulling the empty wagon behind them.'

It sounded an uncomfortable, if not dangerous manoeuvre. Cassandra's enthusiasm for such an expedition waned considerably, but then she reminded herself that a girl who hoped to marry Martin and share his life would not baulk at facing peril and hardship.

'How much money will you need?' she asked.

Brother Daniel did some rapid sums on the scrap of paper. 'I believe seventy-five pounds would answer the case.'

Cassandra nodded, and rose. 'Please wait here for me. I shall not be long.'

In her bedroom, she found Bridget unpacking her night attire. While Cassandra unfolded the roll of banknotes which she had brought with her, she recounted Saul Parnell's arbitrary and mystifying refusal to escort them, and told the maid of her meeting with the two missionaries.

Dubiously, Bridget eyed the pile of banknotes which Cassandra was counting out. 'Are you sure they're to be trusted entirely, Miss Cassandra?'

'Well, of course! They're *missionaries*!'

'But Apostolics,' Bridget said darkly.

Cassandra laughed. 'Oh, I see!'

The maid's fears proved groundless, for by the evening Brother Daniel and Brother Alan returned to the Carlton, and the elder missionary scrupulously returned to Cassandra six pounds, seven shillings and threepence-three-farthings, being the unspent balance of the seventy-five pounds

They had bought everything necessary, and would be ready to move on in the morning.

'*Give not sleep to thine eyes*,' Brother Daniel quoted jovially, '*nor slumber to thine eyelids*. Brother Alan and I shall be spending the night in packing and preparing for the expedition.'

Cassandra did not see the Blue-Eyed Induna again. In the morning, Brother Daniel drove the wagon, drawn by a span of twelve oxen, to the front entrance of the Carlton and Brother Alan assisted in packing Cassandra's luggage on the vehicle. Then, after a brief prayer led by Brother Daniel for the safety and success of their expedition, they set off.

Brother Alan rode one of the horses and led the other, while Brother Daniel cracked the long whip over the oxen from the driver's seat. The lumbering beasts, with their fearsome-looking horns, were surprisingly tractable—all but one of the leaders, whom Brother Daniel nicknamed Malachi. This particular bullock had a stubborn will of its own and had continuously to be restrained from following a path of its personal choosing.

By nightfall they had left D'Urban behind them, and made camp. Brother Alan went out foraging, and returned with pineapples which he had cut from plants growing wild. These, supplemented by bread, cheese and pickles, formed their evening meal.

With the horses knee-haltered to prevent their straying, and the two leaders among the oxen yoked for the same reason, they settled down for the night. The missionaries slept, rolled in blankets, beside the wagon while Cassandra and Bridget were slightly more comfortably ensconced beneath the canvas of the wagon itself.

This set the pattern for the days which followed. They travelled along a route which led ever upwards, from plateau to plateau. Below them a panorama of hills lay spread out beneath the sub-tropical sun.

On the fifth evening, when they had made camp as usual, Brother Daniel said with satisfaction, 'Two more days, my dear Sister Cassandra, and you will be safely in the care of your cousin Martin.'

Her heart bumped. They would be reunited by Christmas after all! She smiled at Brother Daniel with gratitude and affection. 'You and Brother Alan will, I trust, stay over at Magwana for a while as our guests?'

'That's very kind, my dear. We should welcome the chance of hearing about your cousin's experiences.'

Cassandra awakened in the morning to sunlight pouring in a molten gold shaft into the canopied wagon. She sat up with a start. It must be quite late for the sun to have so much strength, and Brother Daniel always preferred to make an early beginning to their day's travel. Bridget, she noticed, had already risen and left the wagon.

Cassandra was pulling her gown over her shift when the flap of the canopy lifted, and Bridget's set, freckled face appeared.

'They've gone,' she said baldly.

'*Gone?*' Cassandra stared at her. 'What do you mean? Who, and what, have gone?'

'Them two catchpenny preachers, that's who.' Bridget's voice was grim. 'Likewise the horses, Miss

Cassandra, and heaven knows what besides. You'd best see if your money's safe.'

The money was not in the valise under the driver's seat where Cassandra had been keeping it. Instead, she found a note addressed to her.

'Dear child, our need is greater than yours, and as the Good Book says—The Lord helps those who help themselves. Brother Alan and I, do you see, have a notion to save a few souls at the diamond mines of Kimberley, and one or two technicalities—not unconnected with the law—precluded us from travelling there by the direct route. To have left you closer to Magwana would have taken us too far out of our way, but by my reckoning you are no more than four days away from the mission, provided you keep going due east.

'You will see that we have left you a fair share of the provisions, dear child. You have watched how we hitch the oxen to the wagon and should have no difficulties there.'

The outrageous missive ended piously—*'May the Good Lord be with you on your journey, and keep you safe.'*

'Well!' Cassandra breathed on a note of outrage and helplessness.

Bridget became practical. 'We'd best see and hitch the beasts to the wagon, Miss Cassandra.'

The task occupied most of the morning. Except for the two leaders, the oxen were docile and manageable enough, and walked placidly to their allotted places in the shaft. But Malachi, particularly, took full advantage of the absence of the two men. He would wait while the girls approached him, and take to his heels at the last moment. But eventually they caught him off guard and pulled him, furiously bellowing, towards the wagon. Only the yoke restrained him from butting them with his murderous horns.

They did not cover much ground that day. The two

leading oxen recognised lack of authority when they met it, and stubbornly refused to do either Cassandra's or Bridget's bidding. By the time they made camp that evening Cassandra was not sure if they had been maintaining an easterly course.

It took slightly less time, the next morning, to subdue Malachi and hitch him to his co-leader in front of the wagon. But he extracted his revenge by being more unco-operative than before, and leading the wagon through dense, high thorn scrub.

By the third morning since the defection of the two 'missionaries', no one could have told the difference in social positions between Cassandra and Bridget. Both girls were exhausted, grimy and dishevelled. Cassandra's costume was no longer remotely smart, and her best bonnet hung in flaps of torn and grubby straw about her head. Were it not for the slight protection it offered against the scorching sun, she would have thrown it away.

There was no water near the place where they had made camp the night before, and they could not afford to sacrifice any of their drinking water for washing. So they dressed, made a hasty breakfast, and set out to hitch the oxen to the wagon.

But this morning Malachi had surpassed himself. They had evidently not secured the yoke properly about his neck the previous evening, for he had somehow divested himself of it, and each time they tried to draw near to him he lowered his horns in a menacing fashion. Then, suddenly, he decided to vary the vindictive game he was playing with them. As they approached him, he turned and lumbered away through dense undergrowth.

Cassandra was desperate, and close to tears. 'We can't move on without the leaders,' she told Bridget. 'The other oxen won't budge without them. You hitch the others to their traces as best you can, while I try to round up that devil!'

Malachi continued with his tactics of waiting until Cassandra was gingerly approaching, and then taking to his heels, afterwards repeating the whole infuriating process all over again.

Sobbing and breathless, Cassandra blundered after him with dogged despair and not the slightest hope of subduing him.

She stopped, blinking through the tears and rivulets of perspiration which were blinding her. A figure had appeared in Malachi's path as if he had sprung up out of the ground. Cassandra had only time to register the fact that he was tall and powerfully built, with skin like gleaming black satin, and that he was wearing an elaborate headgear of otter skins and feathers, with strips of animal pelt around arms and ankles. Then Malachi, charging with head down, had struck the man a glancing blow, hurling him to the ground.

Cassandra covered the distance between them in a stumbling run. The man had sat upright and was examining a wound in his upper arm. She sank down beside him, and took his arm in her hands.

'Oh, I am so sorry! That *brute*—I wouldn't have had this happen for anything! Let me see if I can stop the bleeding . . .' It did not occur to her until later that he wouldn't be able to understand a word she said.

While she had been talking she had ripped the edge off her petticoat, and was dabbing at the wound. Fatigue and despair, followed by shocked surprise, had rendered her completely fearless.

A sound to the right of her made her look up. Malachi's triumph had turned his head, for he was pawing the ground, and making it clear that he intended charging again, deliberately this time.

Cassandra acted with the primitive, female instinct to

protect the weak or the injured. She pushed the wounded man to the ground, and crouched over him, making herself as small as possible and praying.

Something whistled through the air. The sound was followed by a dull thud. When she raised her head cautiously she saw that Malachi was lying on his side, his eyes rolling, with some fearsome kind of spear piercing his body. The next moment her blood ran cold.

Where there had been nothing but bush and scrub and outcrop of rock before, there was now suddenly a horde of black bodies, all resplendent in feathers and animal skins, armed with shields and long, slender spears.

She cast a hunted look about her for a way of escape. But a hand encircled her arm, and she turned to look at the wounded man.

'Do not be afraid,' he said in perfect English. 'My people would not harm a defenceless woman. Why are you here alone?'

'I—I want to join my cousin at Magwana. My—servant and I—we were cheated by our guides, and abandoned . . .' She brushed tears of shock from her eyes. 'And now our leading ox is dead . . .'

'Your wagon is—where?'

'In that direction.' Cassandra pointed a trembling finger.

The man rose, holding out a hand to help her up. 'Go back to your wagon and wait. I shall send someone to take you to Magwana. It may take a day, perhaps two.'

She looked uncertainly at the surrounding mass of what she now guessed to be warriors. 'Will—will we be safe until then?' she stammered.

The man turned his head, and called out something which she could not understand. A young, graceful girl wearing an astonishing assortment of beadwork upon her body and little besides, moved statuesquely through the armed warriors towards Cassandra's companion.

At a word from him, she removed one of the pieces of beadwork from about her neck. The man lifted it above Cassandra's head, and allowed it to fall about her throat.

'Wear it,' he said. 'It is my gift to you. It will keep you safe.'

Then, as swiftly and silently as they had appeared, all of them vanished into the undergrowth again. After a few minutes of stunned disbelief, Cassandra picked her way back to where Bridget was waiting with the wagon and the rest of the now useless oxen.

When Bridget had heard the whole story, she looked dubiously at the beadwork about Cassandra's neck. 'Nasty, heathen thing,' was her opinion. 'Will you do as the man said, Miss?'

'There's nothing much else we *can* do. These oxen have been trained to follow a leader, and without the wretched Malachi they would pull us in all directions.'

Bridget was still unhappy about the beadwork. 'How can it keep you safe, Miss Cassandra? If you want my opinion, there's something pagan about it. Like witchcraft.'

'I dare say he only said it to reassure me.'

While they waited with the wagon, both Cassandra and Bridget became increasingly grubby. If anything, the maid presented a better appearance than the mistress, for her plain gown did not look as noticeably dishevelled and dirty as Cassandra's finery. And her carroty hair, in their accustomed braids, was decidedly more presentable than the ruins of Cassandra's elaborate coiffure.

A day and a half later they were trying to find shelter in the meagre shade cast by the wagon when a cloud of dust appeared on the horizon. It was a male figure on horseback, driving two oxen before him.

As he approached, Cassandra saw, with an unwelcome shock, that it was the Blue-Eyed Induna.

He jumped from his horse, and regarded her with grim disfavour. 'If I were not bound by orders from the king, Miss Hudson, and if you were not wearing his personal guarantee of safe conduct about your throat, I would leave you here to rot.'

She flushed, and then frowned. 'The King?'

'Cetewayo. *Nkosi Kosi*. King of all the Zulus.'

Her hand went to the beadwork about her neck. *That* had been King Cetewayo, the man whom Colonel Thesiger had described as a murderous tyrant, an ignorant savage who had to be taught his place?

Then she became aware that Saul Parnell's disparaging glance was looking her up and down, and she drew herself erect with as much dignity as she could muster. The effect was somewhat spoilt when a flap of her ruined bonnet fell across her eyes, momentarily blinding her.

He pushed the bonnet back upon her head, looking at her with cynical amusement.

'Not much left of the Parisian bonnet, is there, Miss Hudson,' he drawled, 'with which to impress those poor heathen children?'

CHAPTER
TWO

SAUL PARNELL experienced a perverse satisfaction at the girl's humiliation. His contempt for meddling missionaries who rode roughshod over people's traditions in their quest for converts, was matched only by the scorn he felt for fashionable females who came to play Lady Bountiful.

Teach the poor little heathen children to read, indeed! Read *what*? Elementary English, of course; cat-sat-on-the-mat stuff, of no relevance whatsoever to their lives. No matter that they had a language and a culture of their own, a rich imagery of expression and a vocabulary not far short of Shakespeare's. The arrant conceit of the girl!

He watched a slow flush stain her cheeks, and saw the angry glitter of her eyes. 'Mr Parnell,' she said, tight-lipped, 'I wish King Cetewayo had sent anyone but you to escort us to Magwana!'

'Miss Hudson,' he returned with an ironic bow, 'you do not wish it more than I do. However, the King felt you would be more comfortable travelling with some-one who spoke your language. Now, I suggest that we lose no time in getting started, so that we may take our leave of one another as soon as possible. Kindly round up your oxen.'

Cassandra stared at him in fury. He had thrown himself down on the ground in the shade of the wagon, and was making it clear that he had no intention of helping with the rounding up of the oxen. She was about to make a blistering remark, but something like a challenge in those intensely blue eyes stopped her. Instead she muttered to Bridget, and the two of them fanned out to drive the oxen to the wagon.

Parnell folded his arms behind his head, and moodily watched the two girls. Perhaps he was unfairly visiting on Cassandra Hudson the anger he felt with the British government, simply because she seemed to embody everything that was arrogant and ignorant and condescendingly righteous about the British.

His mouth twisted in a slight smile. There he went again, forgetting that he was himself British. Although in truth, he did not forget it nearly as often nowadays as he used to. As he grew older, his sense of being a hybrid, of having each foot in two different worlds, increased.

He sighed, and rose. The sooner he delivered the little bedraggled fashion plate to her bigoted cousin at Magwana, the sooner he could set about trying to resolve the dilemma which faced him.

Swiftly, he helped the girls to hitch the oxen to the wagon, and to break up the camp. Bridget lingered for a moment afterwards, to stroke the muzzle of Saul Parnell's fine roan mare, crooning softly to the beast.

He raised his eyebrows at her 'You know something about horseflesh, don't you?'

'Indeed I do, sir.' She bobbed a curtsey. 'In Ireland, when I was little, me Da' had the care of the Master's stables, and I learnt to ride early——'

'You're Irish!'

Again Bridget curtsied shyly. He began to question her about her memories of Ireland and of horses.

Cassandra had been watching and listening with a jaundiced expression. The man could be civil enough to Bridget, it seemed, while she herself earned nothing but his scorn. She turned her back on them, and climbed under the canopy of the wagon, tacitly taking it for granted that Bridget would be driving the wagon, as she had been doing since the two 'missionaries' decamped.

Cassandra had barely found a comfortable position before the wagon flap lifted, and Saul Parnell's head appeared.

'Out,' he said briefly.

'Why?' She glared at him, gritting her teeth.

'You'll have to lead the oxen.'

'*Lead* them———? They did not need leading before!'

'They will require leading now. We are not far from the Tugela River Valley, and the terrain will be changing. They will need to be kept to a track.'

Bridget's face appeared in the flap opening too. 'I'll lead them, Miss Cassandra,' she offered, 'while you drive———'

'No,' Saul Parnell interrupted. 'I'll do the driving myself. You, Bridget, will ride my mare.'

Involuntarily, Bridget's plain face lit up with joy at the prospect. Cassandra told herself that if he had acted out of kindness to the maid, she would have applauded his thoughtfulness. But as it was she tried to stifle her anger, for she guessed what his purpose was. Bridget, the maid, was to ride in style while she, the mistress, was to lead the oxen. It was another attempt to humiliate her.

She stared defiantly at him. His calm blue gaze held hers, asserting his authority, making it plain that as an Induna he was accustomed to being obeyed. Cassandra was the first to drop her eyes.

Her face set, she jumped from the wagon and moved to the head of the oxen, taking hold of the rope which coupled the two new leaders. Behind her, the oxen plodded on slowly, the whip wielded by Saul Parnell flicking the air now and again as they stopped to ruminate. Ahead of them Bridget streaked joyfully along on

horseback, untouched by the cloud of red dust which
the ox team was kicking up about Cassandra.

The ground, which had been level and flat for some
time, broken only by occasional stunted trees or out-
crops of rocks, now began to change. Cassandra realised
that they had been travelling along a lofty table-land
some three thousand feet above a riverbed. She stopped
involuntarily, and gazed in awe at the panorama below
them.

The earth fell away, as far as the eye could see, in
serried ranks of peak upon peak, like gigantic jagged
teeth. In places their outlines were softened by wooded
spurs or broken by rocky strongholds. And far below,
in the midst of all this grandeur, the river glinted like an
undulating snake.

Bridget, who had disappeared from view,
materialised through the undergrowth, her face flushed
with enjoyment and exercise.

'Follow me, Miss Cassandra! I've found the track.'

Cassandra nodded, frowning. She had remembered
for the first time what 'Brother Daniel' had said of the
Tugela River—that the provisions would have to be
ferried across on horseback, and the oxen persuaded to
swim to the other side, pulling the empty wagon behind
them. Already the sun was low in the sky, so it seemed
that the operation of crossing the river would take up
most of tomorrow.

With the wagon and oxen lumbering behind her,
Cassandra followed Bridget's tracks in the descent. The
slopes became luxuriously wooded, the terrain down to
the waterside an alternation of gentle, park-like
verdure, steep rugged rock and dense forest. But a
fairly comfortable track had been beaten by previous
travellers, and it was not difficult to lead the oxen
along it.

The Tugela River was wide, fringed in places with

dense reed thickets, its red water creaming over rocks Cassandra came to a halt on the bank of the river. Bridget had halted too, the mare eagerly lapping at the water.

Cassandra thought wistfully of washing the worst of the caked dirt and red dust from her face, then turned her back on the river and walked to the wagon

Saul Parnell looked down at her from the driver's seat. 'Why have you stopped, Miss Hudson?' he enquired. 'Is anything amiss?'

'Amiss? No . . . I've stopped, of course, because we can't go any further without unloading the wagon.'

'Nonsense! What made you suppose that?'

She set her teeth. 'Common sense, Mr Parnell! The oxen would drown if they had to attempt to swim across, pulling the heavy wagon!'

An eyebrow quirked at her in condescending amusement. 'The water here is not deep enough to reach your waist, Miss Hudson. Now go back and take the lead rope, for left to their own inclinations the oxen would refuse to enter the river.'

Cassandra bit her lip. How stupid of her! Of course, 'Brother Daniel' had lied about the depth of the river to explain the need for buying two saddle-horses with her money.

All the same, she glared mutinously at Saul Parnell. 'I *won't* lead them through the water! I've done my share!'

'If I thought you would be able to control the wagon and manoeuvre it through the river without overturning it, I would change places with you.' He turned his bright gaze upon her. 'But perhaps you consider that your maid should lead the oxen, and allow you to cross the river in dignified comfort?'

That was more or less what Cassandra had had in mind, but under his sardonic, challenging gaze nothing

would have made her admit to it. Grimly, she strode
back to the head of the oxen, taking the lead rope in one
hand, and hitching up her skirts with the other. The
sight of Bridget crossing the river ahead of her, on the
gracefully high-stepping horse, did nothing to cool her
temper or lessen her mortification.

Several times Cassandra lost her footing in the fast-
flowing river and stumbled to her knees. By the time
she reached the far bank her clothes were clinging wetly
to her body; she was covered with mud and her arms
and knees were grazed by contact with the rough
boulders in the river bed. Neither her appearance nor
her temper were helped when the leading oxen, in their
relief at reaching dry land, put on a sudden spurt of
speed so that she fell headlong into a thicket of slimy
reeds.

She heard Saul Parnell, amusement in his voice, call
out unnecessarily to her to halt. He jumped from the
wagon.

'You may relax now, Miss Hudson. We'll make camp
here until morning.'

She glared at him through a curtain of hair streaked
with mud and green slime. 'Oh, pray don't consider
me, Mr Parnell! Surely you wish me to pull the oxen up
that crag while there's still light in the sky and breath in
my body?'

His mouth twitched. 'The oxen team needs to
rest and graze,' he said mildly. 'If you and Bridget
will unyoke them, I'll see what I can find for our
supper.'

He picked up his rifle and walked towards the lip of a
forest which fringed a steep, rugged crag looming
beyond the river. Cassandra stared after him.

'Oh, how I'd like to pay him out!' she said wistfully.
'How I *detest* that devil!'

'Whisht, Miss Cassandra!' Bridget protested,

shocked. 'And himself come to rescue us, and every-thing! I'm thinking 'tis a true gentleman he is, for all he was raised a savage.'

Cassandra gave her a sour look. 'You may well think so *You* weren't made to lead those wretched oxen!'

Bridget turned a troubled expression on her. 'Sure, Miss Cassandra, I'd gladly have changed places with you, but the truth was, ye'd never have controlled the mare. A spirited craythur, she is, for all she looks as meek and mild as a milk puddin'. Not that it wasn't a rare treat, riding her . . .'

Cassandra sighed, and placed an arm about Bridget's shoulders. 'I don't really bear you a grudge. Look, I must get out of these clothes and clean myself up while that—while Mr Parnell is out of the way. Could you see to the oxen by yourself?'

Bridget nodded. Cassandra climbed into the wagon and unpacked a gown of white Pompadour sateen sprigged with tiny embroidered flowers, together with a change of underclothing. Then she made her way down-river, and in the cover of a large overhanging boulder, screened by undergrowth from the bank. She stripped to her pantaloons, washing the mud from the rest of her clothes

When she had spread them on the rock to dry, she waded deeper into the river and, to her delight, dis-covered a warm spring welling up, comforting and invigorating. She knelt down, immersing her head in the water until it was squeaking with cleanliness, all the mud and slime washed away.

Cassandra had just straightened up, and was shaking her wet hair over her shoulders, when movement caught her eye. She watched, fascinated with horror, as a reptilian creature broke the surface of the water towards her. She recognised it from numerous visits to

Regent's Park Zoo. It was a crocodile.

Her high-pitched screams seemed to echo along Tugela River Valley, bouncing off the rocky peaks. There was a swift movement through the undergrowth edging the river, and then Saul Parnell's voice cut through her own panic-stricken shrieks.

'*Run for the rock!*'

She turned to obey, and remembered her state of nature. Instinctively she lowered herself into the water and watched, hypnotised and helpless, as the pointed jaw of the crocodile edged closer to her.

'Damn you!' Saul Parnell bellowed from the bank 'I've seen naked females before! *Run!*'

Cassandra let out a sob, and dashed through the water towards the boulder. Parnell knelt down and grabbed hold of her shoulders, pulling her up on to the rock. Then, ignoring her, he cocked his rifle and fired at the crocodile.

Cassandra, trembling violently, pulled the sprigged sateen gown over her head. She turned to Saul Parnell, who was watching the mortally wounded crocodile strike out feebly towards the centre of the river. The enormity of his callousness blotted everything else from her mind. 'You—you made me lead the oxen,' she accused unsteadily, 'and all the time you knew—you *knew* there were crocodiles——'

'I kept my eyes open and my rifle at hand,' he said shortly. 'The river *had* to be crossed. Would it have helped you if you'd known there were crocodiles?'

She could think of nothing sufficiently biting to say in reply to that, and so began to gather together the clothes she had washed, while Parnell recovered a brace of shot waterfowl which he had flung down on the river bank earlier.

As they began to walk towards the wagon afterwards, Cassandra was still shaken by her experience. But suddenly another aspect of it struck her, and she felt the blood rising to her cheeks

With difficulty, she said, 'I—I should be grateful if you would say nothing of what happened when we—when we reach my cousin's mission.'

He nodded, his lip curling. He understood her perfectly. Mealy-mouthed Martin Coleman would be far more profoundly shocked to know that his cousin had bathed in the river in a state of undress than at the news that she had almost succumbed to the appetite of a crocodile What an inordinate fuss the British made about nudity!

And yet ... He glanced at the girl. There was no doubt that her own consciousness of her half-naked body had awakened his awareness of it too, when he daily took semi-nudity in the Zulu maidens about him for granted. He could not help remembering the silky-soft feel of her bare shoulders as he pulled her from the water. With a gesture of irritation, he pushed the thought from his mind

Later, when they sat beside a camp-fire, eating broiled waterfowl and listening to the song of the frogs from the river, he ignored Cassandra and addressed himself to Bridget.

'Tell me about Ireland '

'Well, sir, 'tis a powerful green land——'

'It has a heavy rainfall?'

'It has that, sir.' She glanced shyly at him. 'Begging your pardon, sir, but yourself has never been to Ireland? I'm thinkin', with a name like Parnell——'

'You're quite right, Bridget My paternal grandfather was Irish Indeed, I own estates in County Limerick bequeathed to me by him, but I've never seen them.'

At this Cassandra was sufficiently startled to say, 'You own estates in Ireland, and yet you're content to remain here, living with people who murdered your parents——'

She stopped. He had turned his head towards her, and firelight played upon his face, creating dark hollows and sharp planes and giving him an austere expression.

'Murdered, Miss Hudson?' he repeated. 'Where did you come by that tale?'

'I——' She began, confused. 'It was told to me by an army officer. It seems to be a general belief.'

'Naturally.' There was a heavy irony in his voice. 'Since it comforts the British conscience to see the entire Zulu nation as savage heathens, it follows that their every action should be construed as brutish and barbaric.'

'If your parents were *not* murdered by the Zulus,' Cassandra asked, 'then how did you come to grow up among them?'

'I was six years old when King Cetewayo's men found me wandering in the bush, half-starved, barely alive, delirious. My parents were indeed dead, but they had succumbed to typhoid which had raged through our farm, killing my family and their two servants. I was old enough to realise that I had to get out and seek help from somewhere or I, too, would die——'

'Dear sufferin' Virgin,' Bridget breathed softly, with pity.

Parnell half-smiled at her. 'King Cetewayo's men carried me to Ulundi, the royal *kraal*, where I was nursed back to health. The king's family became my own, his *kraal* my new home and refuge.'

'I see,' Cassandra murmured. 'But—you received an education from somewhere——'

'Indeed,' he acknowledged, his voice expressionless. 'When I was eleven years old an English missionary heard about me, and demanded that I be released into his care. He personally took my education in hand, cramming an intensive course of learning into my head. He meant me to be a credit to him.

'He beat me daily, for my own good,' Parnell went on. 'He taught me that everything I had learnt from the Zulus was wrong and wicked; that the Zulus themselves were wrong and wicked, and that the closest they could hope to get to a state of grace was by becoming as much as possible like the white man.

'I was thoroughly miserable, but I accepted everything I was taught and endured what the missionary called the mortifying of my flesh, for he was a man of God, wasn't he, and therefore he had to be right. And then, soon after my sixteenth birthday, I overheard him discussing with his wife how he would trick me into signing over to him the legacies I would receive from the estates of my parents and grandparents. The money was to be used for a school to be endowed in the missionary's name, so that posterity would know how he had striven to educate and save the poor heathens.'

Saul Parnell smiled faintly. 'The very next day I ran away, back to those same heathens. They welcomed me, and sheltered me, and when I grew older I was able to serve King Cetewayo in many ways. After a time he proclaimed me one of his Indunas and gave me a chieftaincy of my own *kraal*.'

Bridget let out a long sigh, but Cassandra sat in silence, staring into the fire. So that accounted for his jaundiced opinion of all missionaries. But even if one granted that he had suffered at the hands of one particular white missionary, surely there were many things about the Zulu way of life which must stick in the gullet of an educated man such as he was?

She leant forward. 'I know from my cousin's letters, that the sav—that the Zulus *buy* their wives. Surely you don't defend that custom?'

He looked at her. 'And don't you think, Miss

Hudson, that if a man has had to pay dearly for his bride, he would appreciate her all the more?'

'You're trying to confuse me! That is not the point at all! Why, my cousin tells me that the Zulus do not confine themselves to one wife only, but take as many as they can afford, and that the chiefs often have as many as a dozen wives——'

Her voice trailed off. In the silence which followed she was aware that his eyes were amused and cynical on her face

'To answer your unspoken question, Miss Hudson,' he said at length, breaking the silence, 'no, I do not have a dozen wives. Indeed, I do not even have one.'

Cassandra rose abruptly. 'It has been a long day, and I have no wish to prolong it any further. I'm going to bed.' She glanced at Saul Parnell. 'When do you expect to reach the Magwana Mission?'

'If all goes well, and if we make good time, tomorrow evening.'

'Good! I shall look forward to that!'

'So shall I, Miss Hudson,' he returned suavely. 'So shall I.'

Bridget rose too, and accompanied Cassandra to the wagon. Saul Parnell threw another branch on the fire, and stared into the flames.

He had tried to convince Cetewayo that the girls should be persuaded to return to D'Urban. This was not the time for gently-reared white females to visit the country. But the King had personally placed his talisman around the neck of Cassandra Hudson, and his honour demanded that his promise be kept. Besides, King Cetewayo could not accept what he, Saul Parnell, saw as inevitable. The King had a touching and naïve faith in the endurance of over thirty-five years of peace and friendship with the British.

Parnell shrugged resignedly. Well, the girls should

be safe enough at Magwana Mission. Besides, they would be Martin Coleman's responsibility. He himself would deliver them to the mission, and not lose any sleep afterwards in worrying about them. He had quite enough on his mind, trying to decide what to do about the conflict of loyalties which faced him.

Early the next morning, when mist curled like smoke above the surface of the river, the oxen were yoked to the wagon once more, and again Cassandra guided the leaders along the rocky gorge through which the ascending trail ran. Her resentment of the task was banked down by the thought that every tortured step upwards in the fierce heat of the sun would take her nearer to Martin. She blotted out fatigue by picturing their reunion and imagining the tender and tentative conversation which would take place between them when they were alone, the exploring of each other's minds, the unspoken intimacies . . .

She sighed, coming down to earth. If only that ruth less, cynical devil Parnell would give her the opportunity, before they reached the mission, of tidying herself a little! Martin had always had a revulsion for slovenliness in a female, and already her hair was escaping in rats'-tails about her head and her gown was streaked with dust.

She was to be given a respite, after all. Once the ascent through the gorge had been completed, Cassandra saw that they had reached another plateau carpeted in long grass and occasional stunted scrub. The oxen could be given their heads and no longer required leading.

Cassandra retreated inside the canopy of the wagon, and set to work to make the best of herself. She washed superficially, dampening a towel with water from their drinking supply. After she had changed her gown and

pinned up her hair to the best of her ability, she reached
into one of her hat-boxes for her second-best bonnet,
a creation of finely gathered pale blue satin lined
with white, and trimmed with violets and lily-of-the-
valley.

Saul Parnell's eyebrows rose with supercilious
amusement when she emerged from the canopy to take
the box-seat beside him, but he made no comment
on her appearance. Some while later he broke the
silence.

'There you are, Miss Hudson—there is Magwana.
Our brief acquaintance is about to come to an end.'

She followed his pointing finger. Beyond a line of
acacias on the horizon she could make out the squat
shapes of a scattering of thatched huts. Her heart gave a
little bounce of excitement. With the end of her journey
in sight, she could even afford to feel kindly towards
Saul Parnell.

'You speak as if you mean to travel straight on. Surely
you will accept my cousin's hospitality for the night?'

He shook his head, his expression sombre now. 'I
must ride immediately for Ulundi, the Royal *kraal*. All
the Chiefs will have gathered there for the First Fruits
Festival, and I must persuade King Cetewayo to call
together the *i-bandla*.'

'What is that, Mr Parnell?'

'The Zulu state council.' He had turned his head
towards her, but his blue gaze was fixed upon something he could see only in his own mind's eye. 'We must
debate the situation . . .'

He broke off, and placed two fingers in his mouth,
whistling to Bridget who was cantering ahead on the
mare. She wheeled the horse about and returned to the
wagon.

'Ride on to the mission, Bridget,' Parnell said, 'and
rub down the mare for me, would you? Then water her

and allow her to graze. I want her fresh as soon as possible.'

Bridget nodded, glad of the chance to gallop the mare. They watched her plunging through the long grass towards the mission.

The sun was dipping towards the horizon, streaking the sky with unreal, flamboyant colour and touching the horizon itself with red and orange as though it were on fire. Against this flame-bright background Bridget and the mare stood out in sharp relief as she galloped the animal back to the wagon. Something was wrong.

Cassandra's hands were tensely clenched in her lap as she watched horse and rider approaching. Parnell was frowning.

Bridget reined in the mare. 'There's no one there,' she stated baldly.

'What—what *can* you mean?'

''Tis deserted, Miss Cassandra. Never a sign of man nor beast. Aye, and the place has been looted by the looks of it.'

Cassandra stared at her in dawning horror. 'Any signs of—violence?'

'I couldn't say. A clothing chest was hacked open—by an axe, I reckon. A table was all but chopped up. But there's no signs of bloodstains, as I could see.'

Panic rose inside Cassandra, and then transmitted itself into anger, wild and unreasonable. She turned on Saul Parnell.

'Your precious Zulus—*they're* responsible! They abducted my cousin, or worse! Savages—bloodthirsty *savages* . . .'.

He was frowning at her. 'No. They had no reason to molest him. At a guess, I'd say that your cousin abandoned the mission, and that it was looted after he left, by his "converts". The table would have been chopped up for no more sinister a reason than that, to a Zulu, it was of far more use as firewood.'

'Martin would never have abandoned his mission!' Cassandra cried. 'It meant too much to him! Besides, he was expecting me!'

'In all likelihood he'd sent a message for you to wait for him in D'Urban,' Parnell reasoned, 'and the message failed to reach you.' He swore under his breath. 'I was against this venture of yours from the outset! I tried to persuade King Cetewayo to order you to turn back, but he wouldn't listen! I had a feeling you'd turn out to be a damned albatross around my neck!'

Cassandra was not listening. 'Something has happened to Martin—I *know* it has!'

'I'll tell you what I think happened to him,' Saul Parnell said brutally. 'He realised that a full-scale war was about to break out between the British and Zulu-land, and he decided that discretion was the better part of valour. He didn't want to risk being caught in the crossfire.'

Cassandra was momentarily shaken out of her blind panic. She stared at Parnell. 'War? No ... Colonel Thesiger said, a few border skirmishes——'

Again he swore, with helpless anger. 'That's what the British think. They imagine that an impressive display of troops on the border, a few reports from their Gatling guns, will decide the matter. And Cetewayo——'

He passed a hand across his face. 'The King clings to the stubborn belief that the British will withdraw their insulting, impossible ultimatum at the eleventh hour. Both sides are wrong. *I* know that, because I under-stand the reasoning of both sides. And I think your cousin Martin realised it too.'

Cassandra swallowed. 'We—we'd better turn back to D'Urban, and see if Martin really has reached it safely——'

Parnell looked at her, his expression hard. 'No sweetheart, your adventuring days are over. I'm taking you straight to Ulundi. The King has promised you his protection, and that is precisely what you will receive—protective custody in the Royal *kraal*.'

CHAPTER
THREE

CASSANDRA was too preoccupied, too racked with desperate anxiety about Martin, to pay serious attention to Saul Parnell's arbitrary announcement. The important thing, the immediate necessity, was to reach the mission and see for herself whether Martin had left any clues as to what might have happened.

She thought of asking permission to ride Parnell's mare, and going on ahead. But Bridget had said that the beast was high-spirited, and besides, Cassandra was used to riding side-saddle. No, she would only risk being thrown.

Her hands clenched tightly in her lap, she endured the excruciatingly slow progress of the oxen towards Magwana Mission. And after all, there was nothing to be learnt from an inspection of the huts which she had not already known from Bridget.

Martin could either have abandoned the mission, to have it looted after his departure, or—he could have been forcibly removed from it, and the place ransacked in the process.

It had certainly been stripped of anything that could have been remotely useful to anyone. An enclosure, which had obviously been used for keeping chickens, was empty of poultry and coops alike. The cultivated land surrounding the mission, on which mealies had been grown, had been harvested of its still immature crop.

In what must have been the store-room, Bridget

pointed out the clothing chest which had been hacked open with an instrument like an axe. Surprisingly, a supply of good, unused homespun breeches and shirts, intended to fit boys and youths, had been ignored while everything else the chest might have contained had been taken.

'The Zulus would have had no use for those,' Saul Parnell said. 'Female clothing would have been taken for the yardage of useful cloth they contained, but homespun breeches and shirts would have had no value at all.'

He went to inspect the rest of the mission, and Bridget said musingly, 'Waste not, want not. No sense in leaving these here for the termites.' She scooped the breeches and shirts into her arms, and carried them outside to the wagon.

Saul Parnell, having made an examination of the mission, turned his mind to the immediate necessity of supper. The mission had been stripped of anything that could have been edible, and it was not likely that he would find small game in this area for shooting. There was no longer any question, now, of pressing straight on for Ulundi; the oxen would have to rest until the morning.

In a nearby *spruit*, which had served the mission with its water supply, Saul found something which had escaped the attention of the looting Zulus. A crude contraption constructed on the lines of a lobster pot had been left, baited, in the water and when he pulled it up it proved to contain two captive carp.

A fire was built, stoked with what remained of the mission furniture, and the carp grilled over the coals. They ate in silence, preoccupied with their own thoughts.

Of the two alternatives, Cassandra was musing, it would be vastly preferable to be able to believe that

Martin *had* left the mission voluntarily. But it seemed so out of character for him to behave hastily, almost in a panic. To understand what could have motivated him, she would have to understand more clearly the situation which faced the country if Saul Parnell was right.

She leant forward, breaking the silence. 'Mr Parnell, this ultimatum which has been sent to the Zulu king by the British—*why* did you say that it was impossible and insulting?'

He turned his head to look at her, his mouth tightening. 'Because Sir Bartle Frere, the High Commissioner, knew full well that King Cetewayo could not possibly agree to its demands without totally betraying his own people. The ultimatum amounts to an invitation to war by calculated insult.'

Cassandra frowned. 'But why? What are its terms?'

'Broadly, that King Cetewayo should disband his traditional *impis*—his military regiments—for good, and that his people should give up their independence and accept the authority of a British Resident in Zululand.'

Cassandra was trying hard to understand. 'But they must have done something to deserve the ultimatum. I remember, Colonel Thesiger said they had been overstepping the mark——'

Parnell made a growling sound in his throat. 'Oh, the British have grabbed at every straw they could to justify their demands! There was the matter of a border infringement by the sons of a Zulu chief, for which the British are demanding a "fine" of six hundred head of cattle and the surrender to them of the chief's sons. In another border infringement, this time by the British, Zulus detained a party of British surveyors who refused to say what they were doing inside the Zulu boundary. The surveyors were released unharmed, but the British claim that the incident was a serious outrage and should be punished.'

'But—by a *war*?'

'I've told you, the British don't believe it will come to that. They want to invade Zululand and bring the Zulus to their knees, and any excuse will do.'

'I don't accept that!' Cassandra said staunchly. 'Britain only invades a country if it's morally justified!'

Parnell uttered a crack of cynical laughter. 'They invade a country when it suits their own ends! In my personal view, there are three reasons why they are eager to force hostilities on Zululand. In the first place, because all Zulu males are, by tradition, conscripted into the King's army when they reach the age of sixteen, it means that the whites cannot recruit Zulu labour. This has always been a source of irritation to the British.

'In the second place, a court of inquiry has just found in favour of the Zulus in a matter of disputed territory on the border, and the British cannot accept that the land must be handed back to Zululand. They argue, if you please, that the Zulus are a migratory tribe with no settled boundaries—this despite the fact that they have been settled in Zululand since the seventeenth century!'

Cassandra's mouth set mutinously. Totally loyal to Queen and country, she could not accept even the most oblique criticism of either. And this man, this renegade, this *traitor*—was ascribing the most unworthy motives to the British!

'Their third reason, in my view,' Parnell finished, 'is a totally cynical one. The British welcome the outbreak of hostilities, because it will give their troops fighting experience and afford a chance for them to try out their sophisticated new weapons.'

Cassandra rose in an abrupt movement. 'I am going to bed,' she said coldly.

Once rolled up inside her blankets under the canopy of the wagon, Cassandra's mind was far too active to

allow sleep. If only Martin were here, she thought
fervently, to demolish Saul Parnell's perfidious slanders
against the British! If only Martin were here to blister
him with scornful argument . . .

Her mind snapped off the thought. Where *was*
Martin? What if he had been forcibly removed
from the place, perhaps to be held hostage by the
Zulus?

Her nails dug tensely into the palms of her hands. It
was difficult to see of what possible use he could be to
the Zulus. And hadn't Captain Bradley said that the
Zulus would not dare to make matters worse for themselves by harming a British missionary?

Well, then. . . . Assuming Saul Parnell was right, and
Martin had foreseen the country being plunged into a
bloody war: surely he wouldn't have abandoned his
mission and all the people who must have depended on
him, to save his own skin?

Oh, no, no, impossible! Martin was far too courageous `and dedicated for such an ignoble act.
Unless—Yes, unless he had done it to save *her*, Cassandra! Knowing that she was due to arrive in
D'Urban, knowing her impetuous nature, he would
have realised that she would be deaf to all orders not to
join him in Zululand. There had been just one way of
keeping her away from the battleground and that had
been by removing himself from it. So, for her sake, he
had decided to sacrifice the mission and hurry to
D'Urban to meet her and keep her safely there until
hostilities ceased.

And somehow they had missed one another along the
way. What would Martin have done when he reached
D'Urban and discovered that she had set out for the
Magwana Mission after all? He would, she answered
herself, have turned around and come back as speedily
as he could. So, the thing to do was to wait here until he

reached her. There was no sense in turning back to D'Urban herself. In that way they could go on for ever, chasing after one another, always just missing one another.

In the morning, Cassandra had made her plans. She found Parnell boiling water for coffee on the fire; their original food supplies still contained dried rusks, which they dunked in the coffee for their breakfast.

Cassandra levelled her gaze on Saul Parnell. 'The time has come to thank you for your assistance,' she said with dignity. 'You were ordered by the King to deliver us to the Magwana Mission, and you have done so. Please feel free to go your own way now.'

He set his mug of coffee down. 'You have a short memory, Miss Hudson. I said that I was taking you to the Royal *kraal*——'

'I have not forgotten what you said, Mr Parnell. But I have no intention of going with you. I am confident that my cousin will be returning for us within a day or two, and we have sufficient supplies left to last until he arrives. So we shall not be troubling you any further.'

After the short silence which followed, Bridget spoke, her voice doubtful. 'Miss Cassandra, save only for the rusks we have a brew or two of coffee left, and no more——'

'We'll ration what there is, Bridget. We won't starve.'

'But if your cousin should not be returnin'——'

Saul Parnell cut through the maid's argument. 'Don't worry, Bridget. You're coming to Ulundi with me, and that's an end to it.' He turned his head to look at Cassandra. 'Get inside the wagon.'

She rose. 'Mr Parnell, you may be an Induna in this country, with authority over thousands of people, but you have no authority over *me*. I refuse to move from this spot until my cousin comes, and that *is* an end to it!'

He rose too, and shrugged resignedly, and dusted his hands together in a significant gesture. As he advanced purposefully towards her, Cassandra stiffened.

'I am well aware that you are stronger than I am, Mr Parnell, and could heave me bodily on to the wagon! But even you couldn't keep me there! Since Bridget seems to have developed cold feet, I'll take the first opportunity to get away from you and return to the mission, where I'll live on what I can trap in the stream until Cousin Martin comes for me!'

He gave her a measured look. 'Yes?'

'Yes! And no matter how many times you may come back for me, I shall run away again and again, so that you will not get very far from this spot before my cousin arrives!'

He gazed at her thoughtfully, and then shrugged. 'I can see that you mean to plague the life out of me, and delay my return to Ulundi as much as you possibly can. And it is vital that I should reach the Royal *kraal* with all speed. Very well, Miss Hudson, it seems you are calling the tune '

Cassandra was astonished that he had given in so easily, and then triumphant. The Blue-Eyed Induna, she thought, had been accustomed for too long to blind obedience. Being defied for once would be a salutary experience for him.

He turned to Bridget. 'Will you help me round up the oxen?'

'They're *my* oxen!' Cassandra protested, before the maid could answer.

'I'm requisitioning them.' His voice was cool, his eyes mocking as they rested on her. 'Perhaps you don't realise how very valuable they are in Zululand They could buy me at least two brides.'

She glared furiously at him. 'You're no better than a

common thief!'

He shrugged, impatient and no longer mocking. 'Your cousin, when he arrives as you so confidently expect him to, will have transport of his own. These oxen will then be an encumbrance. What will you do—turn them loose to take their chances in the wild? Be sensible, Miss Hudson Go and gather together everything you want unloaded from the wagon, while Bridget and I round up the oxen.'

She glared at him for a moment, and then dropped her eyes, moving resentfully towards the wagon. The fact that he meant to unload the vehicle made it clear that he also intended to steal her wagon. Not, common sense told her, that a wagon would be of much use without oxen. All the same, she bitterly begrudged him any of her possessions.

She was under the wagon canopy, looking doubtfully at the meagre food supplies which still remained, when she felt the vehicle tilt slightly under an extra weight, and she said without turning her head, 'Bridget, if you want to go with the man, you're quite at liberty to do so——'

'Indeed, you'll *both* go with the man,' Saul Parnell's calm voice answered her.

Startled, she tried to rise, but she was not swift enough. His arms went around her, pulling her against his chest, while her own arms were pinioned behind her. For the first time she realised that he had a rope.

Cassandra struggled violently, but she was no match for his superior strength. Rage and pride prevented her from giving in, however. A well-aimed kick caught him on the shin and he swore, pushing her to the floor of the wagon. He threw one leg over both of hers, pinning them firmly down while he reached for the end of the rope. Her arms were tied to her sides, her legs trussed together at the knees.

Fury lent a superhuman strength to Cassandra as she raised her helpless body from the waist, her teeth bared to sink themselves into his shoulder. He guessed her intention and, with one hand clasped around her chin, forced her jaws together. Her head fell back on to the wagon floor.

He knelt beside her, his breath coming rapidly. His mouth was curved in a smile, his eyes glittering with triumph and a kind of exhilaration.

'I don't think,' he said, 'that you'll give any further trouble until we reach Ulundi.'

'I hate you,' Cassandra ground out between her teeth. 'Oh, how I *loathe* you!'

He merely continued to smile, and reached for a pillow, pushing it under her head. Now Cassandra saw for the first time that in the struggle the bodice of her gown had been ripped in a long, jagged tear from neckline to waist.

The sight of her ruined gown was the last straw, and set the seal on her feelings of pain, outrage and fury. She began to weep.

'You m-monster!' she sobbed. 'It wasn't enough for you to t-trick me, and offer me violence, and abduct me. . . . You also had to rip my gown, and it was from P-Paris, the very latest Du Barry F-Florentine . . .'

While her answering violence had merely spurred him on, her tears disconcerted him. He dabbed helplessly at her cheek with the edge of the pillow. Then, with clumsy fingers, he examined the torn satin-surfaced silk of her bodice.

'Don't cry. I daresay it will mend.'

'It will *not*!'

'Look—the edges fit together perfectly, see?' He was smoothing the material with his fingers, moulding it to the shape of its former décolletage.

Abruptly, his touch ceased to be mechanical and

comforting, and took on the awareness of desire. He pushed himself backwards away from her, and said tersely, 'I'll send Bridget to you. Don't try to persuade her to untie you.'

Bridget was shocked at the sight of her mistress trussed up like a chicken, but she clearly considered that Saul Parnell had had no alternative. Her approval of the man was becoming intensely irritating to Cassandra.

Shortly afterwards, the wagon began to jolt and sway across the plains while Cassandra, helpless and humiliated, lay tied up beneath the canopy. When they stopped at noon for the oxen to rest and graze, Parnell allowed her hands to be untied so that she could drink a mug of coffee, but it was not until late in the afternoon, when he judged that there was no longer any danger of her trying to make her own way back to the Magwana Mission, that he removed all her bonds and allowed her to climb, stiff, aching and furious, on the box seat beside him.

'You'll pay for what you've done,' she told him vengefully. 'Martin will follow our tracks from the mission, and come after us. And I shall lay a charge against you, Mr Saul Parnell, which will not do the cause of your precious Zulus any good at all!'

He turned his head to glance at her. 'I'm afraid I don't share your utter confidence that your cousin will return to the mission to look for you.'

She was instantly alarmed. 'What do you mean? Do you believe he might be a prisoner after all, or perhaps—worse?'

'No, I do not.' His tone was irritable 'But from what I know of Martin Coleman he is far more likely to pray for you from a safe distance than endanger himself. He would leave you in the hands of the Lord, and then if anything did happen to you, that would be God's will, wouldn't it?'

'I won't listen to your infamous slanders!' Cassandra cried, clapping her hands to her ears.

Saul Parnell shrugged, and gave his attention to his driving.

In spite of herself, Cassandra was stirred by her first sight of Ulundi. The Royal *kraal* was embedded in a deep ravine, approached through rocky defiles. On the right it was protected by the Black Umvelosi River, and on the left by its sister river, the White Umvelosi.

The *kraal* itself was some five hundred yards in diameter, fenced with dry stake and head-high wattle which provided an almost impenetrable barrier against invaders. This fence was closely hedged by an *abattis* of prickly pears and bush thorns. Inside the fence stood an enormous ring of beehive-shaped huts encircled by rush or timber palisades.

Smoke curled from holes in the thatched roofs of the huts, drifting like an opaque mist in the evening air. A confusion of people milled around the ox-wagon as it entered the *kraal*; within moments the oxen were unyoked and herded towards an animal enclosure in the centre of the *kraal* and the wagon pulled up against the *abattis*.

Saul Parnell was talking in an astonishing tongue-clicking staccato to someone. When Cassandra's eyes became accustomed to the pungent wood-smoke in the air she saw that he was addressing a young Zulu girl The latter was tall and shapely, with graceful features Over brow and cheeks her face was smeared with red clay, and her hair had been arranged in a circular cage-like structure upon her head, the whole decorated with intricate beadwork She wore a sheet of coarse brown-ish cloth draped gracefully about her waist, with a necklet and bracelets of animal teeth and small bones, and more beadwork around her ankles.

The girl responded to Saul Parnell in the same staccato clicks, and then signalled to Cassandra and Bridget to follow her.

'Go with Esara,' Saul Parnell said.

'No.' Cassandra's mouth set mutinously. 'I demand to speak to the King! I insist on being sent back to Magwana——'

'At Ulundi,' Parnell informed her gently, 'females do not *demand* or *insist*. And you cannot see the King unless he sends for you. Now go with Esara to the women's hut'

Infuriated and helpless, Cassandra watched him disappear in the smoky mist. Bridget was tugging at her arm. 'Come, Miss Cassandra, we'd best go with the girl-savage.'

The section of huts to which the girl, Esara, was leading the way appeared to be occupied only by women and young children. Curious eyes followed Cassandra and Bridget and small children ran inside doorways to hide as the white strangers passed with Esara.

The Zulu girl stopped outside one of the huts and shyly beckoned to the newcomers to enter. Inside, Cassandra found the floor to be smooth and hard as glass, and she learnt afterwards that it was constructed of earth taken from anthills, mixed with animal blood. A wood-fire had been laid at one end, and the hut's only furnishings consisted of what were obviously sleeping mats of woven grass, and thick, silky-smooth animal skins to serve as blankets

Esara left them there, and Cassandra sank down on to a pile of the animal pelts. 'This is outrageous, ridiculous! I *must* speak to the King——'

She stopped. Esara had returned, wearing the most startling headgear either of the girls had ever seen. This proved to consist of three large calabashes, or dry gourds, stacked one inside the other. Esara removed two of the calabashes from her head and handed them to the girls, beckoning them to follow her.

Cassandra realised that they were to join a procession of women, each with a calabash upon her head, down to the river. It was useless to try and protest when no one understood English, and so, resignedly, she fell into step with Bridget in the procession, the two white girls carrying their calabashes in their hands.

Once the calabashes had been filled with water from the river, however, they proved impossible to carry by hand, for their sides were smooth and slippery and they lacked anything which could have served as handles. The Zulu women, with astonishing grace and dignity, centred their full calabashes upon their heads and proceeded to walk with lithe, swaying movements away from the river. Bridget, with her hair parted in the centre and worn in braids, found it comparatively easy to balance her calabash upon her head while holding it steady with both hands, but Cassandra's abundant curls, pinned to the top of her head, made the operation quite impossible

To her humiliation, her utter inability to carry a calabash upon her head evoked from the Zulu women a kind of amazed sympathy, as if she were a freak, a woman somehow incomplete. They clicked their tongues and shook their heads as they circled her, eyeing the top of her head and offering suggestions in Zulu. At length Esara motioned to her to leave the calabash of water by the riverside and mimed that she herself would return for it

'I'd like to *kill* Saul Parnell!' Cassandra fumed, when she and Bridget had returned to the hut allocated to them. 'I can't live like this; I won't! Not even for a few days!'

'Whisht, Miss Cassandra,' Bridget soothed. 'Sure,

'tis no use beating your head against a wall.'

Esara returned with Cassandra's calabash of water, followed by a second Zulu woman bearing a cooking pot and other crude domestic equipment. A large piece of raw meat was brought into the hut, together with dry corn and a pestle and mortar. By means of mime, it was demonstrated to Cassandra and Bridget that they were expected to grind the corn and boil it with some of the water, and at the same time broil the meat over the fire, which had by now been lit by Esara.

'I won't do it!' Cassandra muttered mutinously, blinking in the smoke. 'We have some rusks left on the wagon; we'll eat that.'

'Indeed, Miss Cassandra,' Bridget said, 'I'm thinkin' this is not meant just for ourselves' supper. From the way of the savage-girl's noddin' and jerkin', it seems to me some kind of ceilidh is to take place yonder, by those large huts, and the food is maybe meant as part of the feastin'.'

Cassandra considered. That put a completely different complexion on the matter. She had noticed that some of the huts were larger than the others, and decorated on the outside with patterns in clay. It seemed probable that these were the royal huts. And hadn't Saul Parnell mentioned something called the First Fruits Festival?

If there was to be a celebration, the King would be at its focal point. She would have the chance to approach him and explain to him that his over-zealous Blue-Eyed Induna had brought her here against her will, and that she wished to depart as soon as humanly possible.

She submitted to being instructed in the art of grinding corn and thereafter transforming it into a kind of boiled spoon-bread. Under Esara's supervision she and Bridget broiled the meat. The smell of the latter reminded Cassandra that she was hungry, and that she had not tasted red meat for several days. She tried to detach a small piece for herself, but Esara stopped her with exclamations of horror. Apparently it was not done to start eating before the feast.

When the food was ready Esara helped them to carry it towards the larger huts A crowd had gathered here, and in the glow of several fires Cassandra could see that some kind of ceremony was taking place. Esara motioned to them that they would have to wait on the periphery of the crowd until the ceremony came to an end.

Cassandra watched, fascinated in spite of herself. Even in the poor light she recognised King Cetewayo, seated in the centre of the circle. He was resplendent in bead decorations, and wore a kilt made of monkey-tails and the skins of civets. His headgear was an elaborate construction of otter skins surmounted by red and white feathers, and around his wrists he wore gauntlets of ox-tails.

Squatting in a circle around King Cetewayo were what Cassandra took to be some of his warriors. Firelight glinted on oiled skins resembling black satin; their plumed head-dresses danced with every movement they made, and the white shields which they held in their hands threw ominous shadows upon the ground.

A strange, rhythmic chant came from the squatting warriors, swelling and rising to a hypnotic crescendo. Suddenly a figure rushed out from the circle, brandishing his spears and rattling them against his shield.

'*Bayete Nkosi!*' he roared his allegiance to his king, and the crowd took up the salutation as if with one voice.

'*Bayete! Nkosi yama Kosi! U-ZULU!*'

Something about the ceremony—its mystical fervour, its single-minded dedication, coupled with the fearsome appearance of the warriors—turned Cassandra's blood a little cold. And then she told herself—It's play-acting, that's all. Dressing up and play-acting.

The ceremony was over. The King withdrew to the doorway of one of the large huts and the warriors seemed to sort themselves into groups. Esara pointed to a semi-circle of some twelve or fourteen men and signalled that the girls were to join them with the food.

Cassandra was so intent upon keeping the King within her sights that she did not realise, until Esara's hand on her arm motioned her to stop, that they had been approaching the figure of Saul Parnell, seated on a skin-covered bench, and surrounded by what were obviously his fellow Indunas.

Perhaps she would not have recognised him immediately in any case, for now he wore the regalia of a Zulu warrior chief, the muscles of his tanned skin rippling below the armlets of civet pelts, the feathers in his head-dress throwing sinister shadows over his face.

Esara had placed her own cooking pot on the ground, and was kneeling by it, gesturing to Cassandra and Bridget that they were to emulate her.

Cassandra looked down at her prostrate figure, and said loudly, 'No, I won't! I won't sit in the dirt to eat my food like an animal!'

'*You* are not expected to eat.' Saul Parnell's voice shook with suppressed laughter. 'The women do not eat until the men have had their fill. You are expected to wait on me with the food, and afterwards you may retire and share what is left between you.'

Cassandra thought of everything she had already endured, and of the meal which she had helped to cook in that smoke-filled hut—all in the expectation of joining in a feast and gaining the ear of the King.

And then she looked at Saul Parnell, whose mocking

grin combined with his warrior regalia gave him a satanic look. Her glance took in the prostrate figure of Esara, humility in every line, as the girl scooped a container full of *amasi* or sour-milk curds from a calabash and respectfully held it out to Parnell.

Very deliberately, Cassandra picked up the still-hot piece of broiled meat and hurled it at the Blue-Eyed Induna. It caught him on the side of the head and then bounced off the calabash of *amasi*, spattering sour-milk curds over him like a snowstorm.

An awed hush fell upon the crowd. Saul Parnell rose, strangely dignified in spite of the specks of milk curd which covered him.

'You fool,' he said quietly. 'You have just publicly insulted one of the King's Indunas, and therefore by implication the King himself. You'd better pray that I'm able to save you from the consequences of your own folly.'

CHAPTER
FOUR

SAUL PARNELL had barely finished speaking when several angry elder women sprang forward, grabbing hold of Cassandra's arms. He addressed them in their tongue-clicking dialect; they replied politely but inexorably and the crowd grunted its approval of the stand they were taking. Saul shrugged, and did not try to intervene again as the women began to force Cassandra towards one of the huts.

He turned to Bridget. 'Go with your mistress. Stay with her, and try and persuade her not to offer foolhardy resistance. It will be difficult enough for me to try and repair the damage she has already caused.'

He strode rapidly towards the Royal *kraal*. King Cetewayo waved aside the women of his household who had been waiting upon him with their cooking pots, and motioned to his Blue-Eyed Induna to take up a privileged position at the King's feet.

'Majesty,' Saul said gravely, 'I am here to ask clemency for the English girl, Cassandra Hudson. She is ignorant of our ways.'

The King gazed at him in surprised reproach. 'And are our ways so different then from her own, my son? Would she have assaulted one of her Queen's Indunas in the same way, in full view of all the people, and expected clemency? No, I do not think so. She has committed a deliberate profanity against one of my chiefs, and I have decided what the punishment shall be. She must receive a public whipping.'

'She did not intend profanity, Majesty. I understand

why she acted as she did——·

'What you understand is not to the purpose. The *people* will understand only that an Induna has been insulted, and that punishment must follow.'

As so often of late, Parnell was made aware of the division between his own inherent culture and that of the people he had adopted as his own. Really, he thought irritably, why *should* it go so completely against the grain to contemplate a Zulu punishment for the English girl? For a similar offence in her own country she would probably be flung into a foul, disease-ridden prison until magistrates could debate what her punishment should be, whereas here at Ulundi retribution would be swift, sharp and clean.

He addressed Cetewayo again. 'The girl did not realise that it was considered an honour for her to be allowed to wait upon me with food, Majesty. She thought, instead, that she had been deliberately humiliated——'

The King shook his head stubbornly. 'How can it be considered humiliating for a young woman to wait upon one of my Indunas? No, my son, the people will not understand. She will have to receive a public whipping, and you must arrange for it to be done forthwith.'

From that attitude Cetewayo would not be swayed. After a while Parnell was forced to admit defeat, and left the royal presence to give orders for the public whipping to be carried out.

It would be administered by elected 'queens' of the maidens' guilds, and would be designed to correct, chasten and. hurt the pride rather than the flesh. Indeed, Saul conceded grimly, it would doubtless do Cassandra Hudson a great deal of good to be subjected to the indignity of having her bare legs beaten with rush besoms in public. So why did he baulk at the mere notion?

News of the public whipping had spread through the
kraal, and spectators had ranged themselves around the
spot where these punishments were traditionally carried out. A hush of expectancy settled over the crowd as
Saul Parnell strode towards the hut to which Cassandra
had been taken. An implacable guard of women squatted at the entrance to prevent her escaping, but they
shifted to allow Parnell to enter. Their burning torches
threw sufficient light for him to see the two girls crouching on skins on the floor.

Cassandra rose, and looked warily at Parnell, trying
to hide her apprehension. The hostility of the women
outside the hut, coupled with the atmosphere of anticipation hanging over the crowd, warned her that some
kind of action was imminent.

She moistened her lips. 'What—what is to happen?'

He hesitated. Instinct told him that she would fight
like a demented tigress if she knew the truth. She would
never submit passively to her punishment. She would
resist, and make matters a hundred times worse for
herself. Far better that the beating should take her by
surprise, and shock her into succumbing without a
fight.

'You are to come with me,' he said evasively.

'Why?'

He was searching for some plausible explanation
when another thought struck him and he addressed
Bridget.

'At their first meeting, the King presented your mistress with his personal emblem. Where is it now? Have
you kept it safely?'

The maid frowned. 'Yon pagan necklace, ye're
meanin'? 'Tis somewhere in the wagon, sir.'

'Go and find it, as quickly as you can.'

When Bridget had hurried from the hut, he turned
to Cassandra again, studying her thoughtfully. She

was wearing a mantelet, richly embroidered at the throat in jet and silk, and fringed with fine shavings of chenille.

'Remove that cloak-affair,' he ordered, 'and leave it here.'

'Why?' Cassandra asked again.

'Don't ask so many questions!' He quelled his irritation, and added soothingly, 'There is to be a ceremonial Zulu rite of penance. You will be required to wear the king's beadwork, and all that embroidery would distract attention from it. Come with me now, and don't be afraid.'

Cassandra accepted the vaguely-worded reassurance, particularly as it was linked with that gaudy piece of beadwork which the King had presented to her. She allowed Parnell to take her arm, and walked with him through the crowd.

He led her towards a stout pole which had been embedded in the earth. Flaming torches spotlighted it, as though it were a stage. With rhythmic, dancing movements, four older women approached from the shadows, and before Cassandra realised what was to happen they had secured her to the pole by means of oxhide thongs.

It had all happened swiftly and smoothly, with barely any discomfort to herself, as if it were part of the movements of a ceremonial dance. Cassandra was not at all alarmed; merely mystified, contemptuously amused and a little impatient. She watched as several other women, carrying besoms, performed a crouching dance about the pole, while the crowd chanted.

Parnell was not watching the ceremony. Instead, his eyes were scanning the crowd for Bridget's carrot-coloured head. What was keeping the girl? Already it was almost too late. The chanting was dying down, and in another moment or so two of the 'queens' would bare

Cassandra's legs while the others administered the public whipping.

At that moment he caught sight of Bridget pushing her way through the crowd. He expelled his breath in a sound of relief and hurried to meet her, taking the amulet from her.

A long, ululating sigh rose in the air as he placed the distinctive beadwork about Cassandra's throat. The dancing women with their besoms fell back and were swallowed in the crowd. Parnell strode swiftly to where the King had been watching events.

'Majesty,' he said, a challenge in his voice, 'who in the whole of Ulundi would dare to lay hands upon the girl while she wears your personal guarantee of protection about her throat?'

Cetewayo glared at him for a moment, and then began to drum his fingers against his knees. 'I had forgotten about the amulet. But when I presented it to her, I did not foresee that she would come to Ulundi, and force me to grant her immunity because of it!' He made an angry, impatient gesture. 'Very well, she must be released. See to it, and attend me at my *kraal* afterwards.'

Parnell bowed himself from the royal presence, and hurried to untie Cassandra. 'Let us collect your mantelet,' he said, steering her towards the hut

'What a meaningless and ridiculous charade that was!' she remarked with scorn. Her fingers began to tug at the beadwork about her neck.

'Leave that where it is!' he ordered sharply.

'Certainly not! Ugly, barbaric thing! I will not pander to your Zulu friends' absurd love of posturing——'

'The absurd posturing, as you call it,' he interrupted evenly, 'was the prelude to a public whipping. And all that saved you from it was the King's amulet.'

Cassandra stared at him, shock and outrage gradually

giving way to relief at the ordeal which she had escaped. She would not, however, allow him to see that she treated the information with anything but dignified contempt.

Drawing herself to her full height, she said haughtily, 'A public whipping? I should just like to see anyone lay hands upon me——'

'Don't tempt me, girl,' he warned. 'Even the king's amulet would not protect you from *me*. All those women outside would regard it as my inalienable right to chastise you. You see, they believe you and Bridget to be my newly acquired brides '

'*What*——?' Cassandra began, and then stopped. If the news about the proposed public whipping had shocked and outraged her, this latest information left her momentarily speechless. She could do no more than stare at him

'When I arrived at Ulundi,' he explained, 'with two nubile young girls and sufficient oxen to pay the bride-price for both of them, Esara and the other women jumped to an entirely female conclusion. I did not realise what had happened until you approached me with food this evening. As far as the women were concerned, it was your duty and your privilege to provide a meal for your lord and master.'

Cassandra could feel the blood slowly drain from her face. She was shaking with passion as she began in a strangled voice, 'That is the most insulting—the most degrading—the most *contaminating* suggestion I have ever heard——'

'Which one?' His voice was deceptively mild. 'The suggestion that your price was a mere half-span of oxen, or that you were considered no more valuable than your maid-servant?'

'You know perfectly well! The suggestion that I—that I would allow myself to be linked in that way with *you*—that I might ever stoop so *low*——'

'Yes, I see.' The torchlight streaming into the hut from outside showed a dangerous glitter in his eyes. Then he moved towards Cassandra, and the light was no longer flickering on his face. 'You spoke about contamination. Did you have *this* in mind, perhaps?'

He caught her to him, his hands insultingly practised as they caressed her body, without tenderness, without warmth, but with all the skill of a musician precisely calculating the effect he wished to create. And after her first instinctive struggles against him, Cassandra found herself, to her utter shame, responding to those exploring hands and becoming limp and quiescent at his touch. He pushed her head back as far as it would go and covered her mouth with his own, making a physical assault of his kiss, but again striking a primitive chord of response inside her.

They did not draw apart until they heard Bridget's shocked intake of breath beside them. Cassandra turned away, trying to repair her dishevelled appearance and deeply humiliated by what she saw as her own moral collapse. What would Martin think if he knew? Oh, but he must never know—*never*! She would die of shame. . . .

Without a word to the two girls, Parnell strode from the hut for his appointed meeting with the King. Cetewayo commanded him to sit, and said without preamble:

'The girl promises to be a bad example to those of our women who are already wayward. As soon as the First Fruits Festival is over, she and her servant must be escorted across the border.'

Parnell nodded. 'I have in mind Oscarsberg, near Rorke's Drift, on the Natal side of the Buffalo River. They could safely be left there at the Swedish mission, in the care of the Reverend Otto Wit. But they should

leave without delay. Let me set out with them
tomorrow——'

The King held up his hand. 'All the Indunas must be
present for the First Fruits Festival. Tradition cannot
be broken. The matter will have to wait.'

Saul Parnell hesitated, wondering if it would be wise
to take this opportunity of pursuing what was already a
sore subject between himself and the King. At last he
decided to take the risk.

'By the time the Festival is over, Majesty, the British
will have invaded Zululand——'

'My son,' the King interrupted testily, 'you and I
have discussed the matter until I have grown weary of
it! I have ever been a great and true friend of the British
nation, and I shall reign and die at peace with them just
as my father, Mpanda, did before me.'

Parnell addressed him urgently. 'I have spoken to the
High Commissioner, and seen with my own eyes the
British preparing for war. Have you forgotten the
ultimatum, Majesty? Do you imagine the British will
withdraw their demands?'

'No,' the King returned unmoved. 'They cannot do
so, for that would seem like weakness on their part.
They would lose face. So they will send an impi against
us, and the two sides will be like children playing at *uku
gwaza insema* for a brief while. You understand, my
son? There will have been no loss of honour on either
side, and we shall be friends again, the British and the
Amazulu.'

Saul made a sound of despair. The kind of mock
duelling which the King had described had been used,
in the past, to release inter-racial tension between
tribes, resulting in a face-saving stalemate in which
neither side claimed victory nor conceded defeat. But it
was naïve and laughable to imagine, as the King did,
that the sophisticated British troops would lend them-

selves to such a charade.

Saul Parnell could not help reflecting how little either side understood the other. The British military personnel to whom he had spoken saw the Zulus quite simply and sincerely as blood-thirsty savages, delighting in butchery. They would be astonished and incredulous if they were told how little stomach Cetewayo had for war.

In their own tent, Cassandra was removing the king's beadwork from about her throat. She studied it abstractedly for a moment and then said in a desperate voice, 'I must get away from this place, Bridget!'

'Yes, Mistress, I think you must,' the maid agreed quietly.

'What do you mean by that?' Cassandra rapped, stung by something in her tone.

'Well, Miss Cassandra, I saw you with himself, remember. Fair 'witched, you were, for the moment. And I'm thinkin', the sooner we get you safe with your cousin, the better.'

She and Martin, Cassandra thought a little feverishly, would sit side by side in the evenings, holding hands and discussing spiritual and uplifting subjects. They would plan their future and reminisce about the past, and never, never again would she be rendered helpless by the raw, searing, primitive passion which had almost engulfed her at Saul Parnell's touch.

She thrust the thought hastily away from her, and said, 'We must take good care of the King's beadwork, Bridget. It may well be our passport out of this place.'

She did not see Saul Parnell again for several days, except occasionally in the distance. Her own life, and Bridget's, took on an unreal monotone. During the day the women set about the business of washing utensils in the river, fetching water, cooking, brewing a sour beer based on mealiemeal. In the evenings the men returned from hunting, laden with carcasses of animals, and feasting would resume where it had left off the night before. Songs were chanted; broiled meat was eaten and beer drunk, and then the warriors performed their fearsomely symbolic dances among the smoke of a myriad fires. But Cassandra and Bridget remained on the periphery of all this, merely watching from the shadows.

In the plentiful time left over from their daily chores, the two girls wove hopeless, impractical fantasies of escaping from Ulundi, but Christmas Day saw them still there. As she and Bridget celebrated the occasion in their hut, Cassandra could not help remembering how she had planned and schemed to be with Martin on Christmas Day, and she began to rack her brains in a renewed effort to hatch a workable escape plan.

It was not that anyone watched them, or paid particular attention to see that they did not escape. But they were so noticeable in that *kraal*, with their white skins and Western clothes, that their every move could not help but be observed. And in order to get away, they would need transport of some kind. There were few horses at Ulundi, and none of them readily available. And whereas there were so many oxen in the animal enclosure that a span of twenty-four would hardly be missed, the difficulties of rounding them up and yoking them to the wagon without anyone seeing them were insuperable.

So the dawning of the New Year, 1879, saw the two girls still impotently kicking their heels at Ulundi. Cassandra was beginning to wonder despairingly if anything would happen to alter the tenor of life in the royal *kraal* when a tremendous commotion galvanised the place one afternoon.

Cassandra joined the crowd, thrusting her way to the

front. She lost her balance and almost fell in the path of four Zulus, obviously members of a scouting party, who were escorting a British soldier at spear-point towards the royal huts.

The soldier was of medium height and powerful build, with a strong, craggy face and compelling sloe-black eyes. His blue-and-red uniform seemed slightly incongruous on him, as if he were wearing fancy dress, and his white helmet was tilted sufficiently to show black, crisply curling hair.

He stared at Cassandra. 'A white lady, is it?' he observed in a slow lilting Welsh voice. *'There's* amazing.'

But he did not look amazed. He looked phlegmatic and dispassionate, as if a hard school had honed away all emotion and taught him to accept with impassive and stoic calm whatever life might toss in his path.

The Zulu guard chivvied him along once more, and Cassandra turned away to find Bridget, and discuss with her the implications of the soldier's arrival at the *kraal*.

At a hastily-convened meeting of the *i-bandla*, or state council, Saul Parnell questioned the captured soldier, and translated,

'The British are mustered beyond the banks of the Tugela and Buffalo Rivers. This man, Gwylfa Jones, was one of a scouting party sent across the border. He lost his way in thick mist.'

King Cetewayo nodded complacently. 'It is as I said. The time for the ultimatum does not expire for another seven days. When it does I shall send an impi to meet them, and after a skirmish has satisfied honour on both sides there will be peace and calm in the land.'

Saul's mouth tightened. He turned back to Infantryman Gwylfa Jones. 'How many British battalions are waiting to enter Zululand?'

'Eight,' the soldier replied readily. 'With a ninth in reserve.'

Saul stared bleakly at him. Some nine thousand professional soldiers armed with sophisticated weapons about to sweep into the country! Certainly *now* Cetewayo would abandon his pathetic faith in a show of shadow-boxing!

But when Saul glanced at the King he realised that Gwylfa Jones's reply had meant nothing to him. The man's slow, lilting Welsh voice was as incomprehensible to Cetewayo as a totally foreign tongue.

Something stopped Parnell from explaining the situation to the king and the members of the *i-bandla*. Instead, he stared suspiciously at Jones.

'You're remarkably willing to give information about the British movements. Why?'

The man shrugged. 'If I refused, the Zulus would maybe have me tortured, isn't it?'

'Maybe. But you impress me as a man who would hold out against any degree of torture.'

The sloe-black eyes stared expressionlessly back at Parnell. 'It's very flattering you are in your opinion.'

Saul Parnell controlled his temper. 'I'm wondering if you aren't a British spy, deliberately spreading false information.'

Jones shrugged again. 'I am a common soldier. I hire my body to the British Army for a shilling a day and a ration of hard-tack. My mind and my spirit belong to me. There is a limit to what can be expected of a man's body in return for a shilling a day with stoppages. You asked about the British troops, and the Queen's shilling is not enough to buy my silence when I am hopelessly outnumbered.'

Parnell frowned. This man, with his sing-song voice and oddly poetic speech, was completely unlike any other British redcoat he had ever encountered.

'You don't possess much loyalty, do you?' he enquired.

'No,' Gwylfa Jones agreed. 'Do you?'

'What do you mean by that?'

'When war comes, on which side is it that you will be fighting? I know about you—he they call the Blue-Eyed Induna. You have much valuable help and information to offer both the British and the Zulus.'

Saul turned away abruptly without replying. He wished that the soldier hadn't voiced the question, for he could no longer pretend to himself that he had withheld information about the size of the British troops from the King because he suspected the information to be false. The truth was that he did not know where his loyalty really lay.

He decided on a compromise. 'Majesty,' he said, 'I don't think you should leave matters as they are until the time given by the ultimatum expires. You would be wise to send scouts to the border——'

'Perhaps, perhaps. I will put it to my *Inyangas* and see what they advise. In the meantime, my son, the soldier must be given good treatment and hospitality. While he is here the two white women will clean for him and feed him. See to it.'

Saul sighed faintly, hoping that the *Inyangas*, or witch-doctors, would not increase the King's complacency with their advice. He gestured to the British soldier to follow him, and led the way to the women's *kraal*.

He did not look directly at Cassandra as he said, 'This is Infantryman Gwylfa Jones, of the Twenty-fourth Regiment. Will you please prepare a hut for him, and make yourselves responsible for his meals while he remains at Ulundi.'

She was uncomfortably aware that this was their first face-to-face encounter since the evening of her shameful behaviour. She tried to make her voice hard and disdainful.

'Is he a fellow-prisoner?'

'*You* are not prisoners, if that is what you're implying.'

'No? Why may we not leave, in that case?'

'For reasons of your own protection. It may interest you to know that Zululand is about to be invaded by British troops. War is inevitable and imminent.'

'Oh!' Cassandra voiced the first thought which entered her head, unconsciously echoing Gwylfa Jones's words. 'And on which side will you be fighting?'

He gave her a long, hard look, but did not reply. He turned and walked away. She felt an obscure stab of satisfaction, for he would surely fight on the Zulu side, and that would give her stronger reasons than ever for despising him.

She turned to the soldier, studying him. He wore that same impassive incurious look of before, but surely he must share her frustration at being incarcerated here.

'I expect you would like something to eat,' she said. 'Bridget is just cooking our supper. And while we wait, we can discuss plans for escaping from this place.'

He glanced beyond her, to where Bridget was kneeling by the fire, turning a brace of guinea-fowl on a spit. 'I have no desire for escaping,' he told Cassandra equably.

'What? But—but you *must* want to escape!'

'Why? Your huts are more comfortable than the open veld; roast guinea-fowl more appetising than hard-tack or corned beef. Besides, if I tried to escape they would put a spear through me, or an assegai, whatever. I would be a fool to do it.'

'You would be a coward *not* to!' Cassandra said, outraged.

'Very likely,' he agreed, unmoved.

She bit her lip. 'Well, if you don't have the courage to escape yourself, at least help Bridget and me to get away——'

'Why?' he asked incuriously. 'You are nothing to me.'

Cassandra lapsed into a baffled silence. The man was a complete enigma to her. A common soldier of lowly birth, and probably illiterate, he yet had a strangely lyrical way of speaking, and he was not in the least servile. He seemed utterly self-sufficient and self-absorbed, sure of himself, unconcerned with the needs of others. Not a man to depend or lean upon.

Inside the Royal *kraal*, Saul Parnell had come to the same conclusion about Gwylfa Jones. He had been listening as the King outlined the decision he had reached about the man, and Saul interrupted with a frown.

'No, Majesty. The girls must not be placed in his care.'

'Why not, my son? You agreed with me that they should be taken across the border as soon as possible——'

'Not by Gwylfa Jones. They wouldn't be safe with him. He would abandon them without the slightest scruple if it suited him to do so.'

'Very well. The girls remain until after the Festival, when you will escort them to the border in person. But meanwhile, the soldier will be sent back with gifts for Colonel Thesiger——'

'I understand that he now bears the title Lord Chelmsford,' Parnell interrupted automatically.

The King inclined his head. 'The soldier will take with him some of our best animal pelts as a token of goodwill.'

Saul stifled a groan. By such pitiful means the King hoped to stave off the inevitable! Aloud, he said, 'Will you not at least send with him a scouting party, so that they may learn something of the strength of the British troops?'

Cetewayo said triumphantly and mysteriously, 'I shall do better than that! Tomorrow you will see.'

With that, Parnell had to be content. He had desperately prayed that the King would send a scouting party to the border, for that would have achieved two aims. It would have absolved himself from all responsibility in the matter, and the sight of Zulu scouts would have shaken the British from any complacency they might be feeling.

He thought starkly of the two choices facing him now. If he told King Cetewayo of the overwhelming mass of British troops hovering at the border, the Zulu monarch would almost certainly send impis to ambush the invaders. The consequent bloodbath, the slaughter of people of his own flesh and blood, would rest squarely on Parnell's conscience.

On the other hand, how could he allow Cetewayo to remain in ignorance, a sitting target for nine thousand expert British troops? How could he stand by and see his adopted people mown down by the fearsome Gatling guns of their enemies?

The dilemma which he had dimly foreseen all along was becoming harsh reality. He was hopelessly caught between two opposing loyalties, and destined to play the traitor towards one of them.

CHAPTER
FIVE

Soon after sunrise had dispersed the morning mist the following day, Saul Parnell discovered what King Cetewayo had kept so triumphantly up his sleeve, and his heart cried out in silent pity and grief at the almost childish simplicity and the doomed optimism of the King's plan.

One by one the impis arrived from Nodwengu, the central barracks near Ulundi, to join those already garrisoned in the Royal *kraal*. In their thousands they came, warriors displaying their war regalia, marching in twelve regiments from the fifteen-year-old boys' to the umKhulutshane, whose men were greybeard veterans in their sixties. Undoubtedly impressive they were, with their powerful oiled bodies, their vivid plumes and fur loin kilts, with their long spears stabbing the air and their bare feet beating a tattoo on the ground. They swung their oval animal-skin shields aloft, and momentarily they were transformed into a milling mob of oxen, calculated to confuse the eye of the enemy.

As the rest of the *kraal* looked on in awe, the impis wheeled and formed themselves into a giant circle of concentric rings. Each warrior laid down his weapon and stood silent and still. King Cetewayo called upon his Chief *Inyanga* for 'mooti' or charmed medicine, which was brought to him in a vessel of water. Using a monkey's paw dipped in the fluid, and muttering a monotonous chant, the King walked around both inside and outside the circle, sprinkling the magic fluid on his warriors.

Finally he positioned himself in the centre of the ring. Picking up an assegai, he pointed it, feigning to stab at his warriors. Then with a cry of 'uSuthu!' he flung the assegai over his head towards the circle.

For a split second there was utter silence. It was broken by a concentrated, blood-curdling roar from the throats of the warriors, a fierce expression of patriotism and dedication.

'*U-Zulu! U-Quobolwayo! Bayete! U-ZULU!*'

The ululating sound died away. Cetewayo strode to Saul Parnell's side. 'You see, my son,' he said complacently, 'the British soldier will tell of what he has witnessed. Colonel Thesiger—or Lord Chelmsford, as he is now named—will be warned. He will accept my gift of fine pelts, and ask for fresh talks between our two sides.'

Parnell said nothing, and the King continued, 'Go now, and tell the British soldier what is expected of him.'

Gwylfa Jones was standing with Cassandra and Bridget, and had been witnessing the spectacular drill of the Zulu warriors. Parnell gave him a searching look.

'What did you think of that?'

'I was wondering,' Jones said impassively, 'how many poor British swaddies will stop those assegais before Chelmsford gets his victory.'

Saul suppressed a sigh. 'The King wishes you to return to your battalion. You are to take a wagon and oxen, and convey to Lord Chelmsford a quantity of animal pelts, a gift from King Cetewayo. The King also particularly wishes you to tell Lord Chelmsford of the drill you have just been witnessing.'

'Frighten him off, is it?' Jones returned cynically.

Cassandra stepped forward, and addressed Parnell in a challenging voice. 'Since mine is the only wagon I've seen in the *kraal*, I take it that you propose to make free with it!'

He turned his head warily to look at her. But to his astonishment she did not demand to be sent to the British lines with Jones, as he had expected. Instead, she went on, 'I don't see why you should steal the rest of my belongings as well as my wagon! I want time to sort through my possessions and unload what I wish to keep.'

Parnell nodded, hiding his relief. 'You may have all the time you require. Infantryman Jones will not leave for the frontier until you are through.'

Cassandra touched Bridget's arm. 'Let's go and move our stuff from the wagon.'

The maid was frowning as they walked towards the *abattis* of prickly pears and thorn bushes where the wagon was stored. 'Sure, Mistress, 'tis an uncommon fuss ye're makin'! There's little enough left on the wagon, and none of it of much use to us now. There'll be blankets, and cookin' utensils, and spare yokes and halters and such for the oxen——'

'You're forgetting something,' Cassandra interrupted enigmatically. 'You're forgetting the boys' breeches and shirts we salvaged from the Magwana Mission.'

Bridget's frown deepened. 'I'm not after understandin' you at all, Miss Cassandra! Instead of botherin' with boys' breeches and suchlike, why did you not ask Mr Parnell to send us to the British lines with yon Welsh soldier?'

'Because he would have refused. If he'd had any intention of letting us go with Jones, he would have brought the matter up himself. And it's no earthly use asking Gwylfa Jones to smuggle us out with him, because *he* wouldn't lift a finger to oblige anyone but himself. Asking, and being refused, would have made both of them suspicious. But we'll be on that wagon when the Welshman leaves, for all that!'

'How?' Bridget demanded.

Cassandra hoisted herself up into the wagon 'Let's find those boys' breeches, and I'll explain '

During the following two hours Bridget and Cassandra made many ostentatious and long drawn-out trips between the wagon and their hut. After the first ripple of interest among the Zulu women and children, their comings and goings were ignored. No one guessed that the water-flasks which they carried from the wagon were being returned to it, filled with fresh water, or that broiled meat wrapped in mealie leaves and flat rounds of griddle bread were being smuggled on to the wagon, concealed beneath the girls' clothing.

They had deliberately spun out the unloading of the wagon, so that the Zulu women charged with the task of loading the animal pelts destined for Lord Chelmsford were waiting with barely-concealed impatience to begin. Cassandra indicated that they were to pass the pelts up to her and Bridget on the wagon, and that they would load them as space was cleared to receive them. In this way they were able to hide their food and water behind the pelts.

The operation came to an end just as it was time for the women to collect water for the preparation of the evening meal. Cassandra made anxious calculations in her head, and joined the procession to the river with Bridget at her side. Her delaying tactics had been designed to force Jones to put off his journey until the morning, and now she could only pray that he would not leave so late tomorrow, that all her plans would be frustrated. She was gambling on him leaving before it grew light.

In the meantime she caused a great deal of amuse-ment by stubbornly trying once again, and with complete lack of success, to balance a calabash of water upon her head. Within sight of the huts, and apparently incensed by frustration and by women's laughter, she hurled the calabash to the ground, aimed an angry kick at it and stormed off towards the huts.

It was a display of temper which was witnessed not only by the Zulu women. With satisfaction, Cassandra saw that several men, including Saul Parnell and Gwylfa Jones, had been watching with amused interest.

She marched up to them, and addressed them in furious tones. 'Yes, it's very funny, isn't it! As funny, no doubt, as stealing my wagon!' She turned to Jones, and said with heavy irony, 'I have removed my belongings from the wagon, so you may take possession of your stolen property as early as you like tomorrow morning.'

He said unemotionally, 'Thank you for telling me, Miss. I shall leave this evening, after supper.'

Cassandra turned away, hiding her elation. She could not have hoped for a better stroke of luck. But she and Bridget would have to hurry to complete their preparations.

Some while later, when Parnell called at the white girls' hut, he stopped short in the doorway, astounded by the sight which met his eyes. Cassandra was there alone, kneeling on the floor and staring broodingly into a looking glass. All around her lay a soft cloud of red-gold ringlets; he sat down on one of the animal skins and picked one up automatically, feeling its silky texture between his thumb and forefinger.

Then unreasonable anger rose inside him as he studied Cassandra. Her hair had apparently been hacked off with a knife, and what remained of it was sculpted in unruly curls close to her head, giving her the gamin appearance of an unkempt youth.

'Have you gone quite mad?' he demanded. 'What is

the meaning of this?'

She looked at him in defiant amazement. 'What on earth is it to you? It's *my* hair! And I've decided that I'm sick of being regarded as an amusing freak by the other women because I can't balance a wretched calabash on my head! Bridget felt the same way.'

She indicated two aggressively carrot-coloured braids on the floor. 'She has gone down to the river to dunk her head in the water, for she claims that cutting her hair has made her itch, but it's my belief the foolish creature has gone to have a secret weep for the loss of her braids.'

'And well might *you* weep, too,' Parnell said coldly 'What do you imagine your Cousin Martin will say when he sees you looking like a disreputable street urchin? He'll be shocked to the core of his prim, conventional soul!'

Privately, Cassandra acknowledged that Martin *would* be shocked. She decided to ignore the slight on his character, and echoed with deliberate bitterness, 'Cousin Martin! I dare say that by the time I see him again, my hair will have grown back completely. For you have no intention, have you, of setting us free—and I fancy I know why! We are to be used as hostages. When the British learn from Gwylfa Jones that we are here, they will hesitate to attack Ulundi!'

'You're talking utter nonsense!' Saul retorted. 'You are not prisoners, as I have told you over and over again. And far from using you as hostages, I have every intention of escorting you myself to the Swedish Mission at Rorke's Drift as soon as the First Fruits Festival is over.'

Cassandra digested this information in silence. With the country about to be plunged into war, a neutral Swedish missionary would not wish to involve himself in any way. He would not take the slightest risks with two female British subjects consigned to his care, and would certainly not allow then to try and reach civilisation. She and Bridget would be forced to kick their heels, perhaps for months, at a foreign mission where they understood neither the language nor the customs of the incumbents. It would be little better than being forced to remain at Ulundi. No, their best course was still to reach the British lines, from which they could be sent to D'Urban under the protection of an armed escort.

She asked, changing the subject, 'What brings you here? What do you want?'

Parnell hesitated. He had called on impulse, because all day he had been expecting a demand from Cassandra to be allowed to leave with Gwylfa Jones. When it did not come some instinct had made him uneasy, and brought him to the girls' hut for reassurance. But instinct had been wrong after all; the notion of leaving with Jones seemed not to have entered her head, and it was as well that he should not put it there.

'You seem very upset about your wagon being commandeered,' he lied, 'so I thought I would come and reassure you that you'll be recompensed——'

'Oh yes? With what? Animal pelts? Beads? Let me tell you——' She broke off with a wince, and began to make furious attempts to reach inside the lace ruching at the back of her neck. 'I see now—what Bridget meant—about itching!' she gasped.

'Hold still,' he ordered, kneeling beside her and forcing her to bend her head backwards. She could feel his hand, warm and slightly unsteady, against the nape of her neck.

'There! That won't trouble you further.' He flicked the offending ringlet of hair from his fingers, and she turned her head. Their glances met, Cassandra's volatile, chameleon-like eyes changing colour with her

shifting emotions as she recalled the feel of his hand
against her skin and then despised herself for her
awareness of him.

'You look,' he said, his voice uneven, 'you
look—utterly disreputable—and yet absurdly enchant-
ing . . .'

Her mouth grew soft and tremulous and her lips
parted slightly. Unconsciously she leant towards him
and his hand curled about her chin, tilting it.

When his lips were inches away from Cassandra's,
Bridget's voice from the doorway shattered the spell,
and they moved guiltily apart.

'I'm thinkin',' Bridget said prosaically, ''tis time I
started preparin' the supper.' But in spite of her
matter-of-fact tone her eyes were grim and condemn-
ing, forming an incongruous contrast with the ginger
hair which stood up in raffish spikes about her head.

Parnell left the hut, and when he was out of earshot
Bridget exclaimed, 'Sure, and it's a good thing we're
leavin' this place, Miss Cassandra! Makin' a holy show
of yourself the moment me back's turned——'

'Oh, be quiet, Bridget!' Cassandra snapped, direct-
ing her anger with herself towards her maid. 'I won't be
preached to by you! Anyone would think you were my
elderly nanny, instead of only a few years my senior!'

'I don't have to be a hundred years old, Miss
Cassandra,' Bridget said darkly, 'to sniff black sin when
it's blowin' in me nostrils!'

Cassandra hastened to change the subject. 'Listen,
and I'll explain once more what we're to do.'

As soon as they had eaten a hasty supper, they were to
pad two of their gowns with other clothing until they
roughly resembled human shapes. The dummies would
then be arranged on sleeping mats in the hut, and
covered with blankets. Bridget and Cassandra, dressed
in boys' breeches and shirts, would make a final trip to

the wagon in the failing light, just when everyone else's attention was on their supper, and the smoke from the many fires was at its densest.

If anyone should chance to come looking for them, a glance inside the hut would cause them to assume that the two girls had retired early for the night. And in the morning, similarly, if any of the women wondered why they were not about and came to investigate, it would seem that the white girls were still asleep.

'They consider us so odd, fortunately,' Cassandra finished, 'that they won't give such lazy behaviour a second thought until it's far too late to catch up with Gwylfa Jones. Bless the man for leaving this evening, and giving us an extra twelve hours' start!'

Bridget pushed a hand through her stubby hair, and said wistfully, 'Sure, but I don't understand at all, *at all*, Miss Cassandra, why 'twas needful for us to be shorn like this.'

'Practicality, Bridget. The same reason which forces us to wear boys' clothing. We couldn't possibly have hoped to sneak away, or hide successfully on the wagon, dressed in our abundant petticoats and panniered skirts, and we certainly couldn't have coped with long hair. We shall have to leave our toilette requisites behind, and can you imagine the difficulties it would have posed, trying to dress our hair without pins or ribbons or combs?

'Besides,' she added with a laugh, 'think what a ridiculous figure you would have struck, dressed in boys' breeches and shirt, and with flaming red braids coiled primly in your neck! The entire British army would have sniggered behind their hands!'

Bridget sighed. 'Ah well . . . Maybe it would please the Blessed Virgin to let my hair grow out not so fierce-coloured next time.'

'Come,' Cassandra said briskly, 'let us make a start

on the dummies.'

Everything went according to plan. In the half-light no one spotted two slight figures in homespun moving through the smoke-filled *kraal* to the wagon. Cassandra wore the King's beaded amulet under her shirt, and they carried with them only one change apiece of breeches and shirts. Cassandra spared a wistful thought for the elegant Parisian wardrobe she was leaving behind her at Ulundi.

Their hiding-place behind the animal pelts was cramped, and the smell of the skins overpowering. They lay absolutely still, merging with their surroundings, when they felt the oxen being hitched to the shafts. Cassandra wondered for the first time why Jones appeared to be in such a hurry that he had not waited until the morning, and instead hoped to persuade the oxen to pick their way in the dark.

But it was not, after all, a dark night once they had left the smoke of Ulundi behind. A full moon had risen, bathing the landscape in mellow light. Perhaps Jones knew what he was doing, after all; in this way, he would break the back of the journey during the coolness of night.

As Cassandra peered above the pelts at the receding Royal *kraal*, she found herself thinking, with a disconcerting pang, that she would never see the Blue-Eyed Induna again. Then, resolutely, she closed her eyes and tried to sleep.

It was an uncomfortable night. Bridget slept, but she tossed and turned a great deal, and muttered in her sleep. Cassandra tried not to think of the fact that they would have to remain in hiding for one more day and a night, so that Gwylfa Jones would not be tempted to turn back to Ulundi with them.

When dawn broke the next morning she waited impatiently for Jones to call a halt. Even if they had no opportunity of stretching their legs, at least it would mean a respite from the jolting of the wagon. But the man seemed possessed of superhuman vitality, driven by an overwhelming urge to reach the British lines as quickly as possible, for the oxen trudged on, spurred by the cracking of the long-handled whip.

Cassandra stirred restlessly. 'We might as well eat something now. I don't think he means to stop for breakfast.'

Bridget looked flushed, dishevelled and uncomfortable. She refused food, explaining that the smell of the skins was making her feel sick, but she drank greedily from the water flask.

At last, just before noon, Gwylfa Jones was forced to give the oxen a well-earned rest and the chance to graze. Cassandra heard his footsteps moving away from the wagon, and when she peered out she saw that he was making for a line of trees, and carrying a gun.

'Quickly,' she urged Bridget, 'let's get down and stretch our legs.'

But the maid, who appeared unusually lethargic this morning, declined to leave the wagon. Cassandra went for a short stroll by herself, and hurried back when she heard a distant gunshot. If Jones had found something for his lunch, he would be returning to the wagon to make a fire and cook it.

He did not delay for any longer than was necessary before he continued his journey. Cassandra reached behind the pelts where they had hidden their food, and said, 'Bridget, you really must eat something this time.'

The maid raised herself on one elbow, and said weakly—'Mistress, I fear I'm ailin'.''

'It's only the smell of the pelts——'

'It is not, Miss Cassandra. I—hoped to keep it from you, for more ill-timed it couldn't be. I have been unwell since soon after we hid on the wagon, and I have been feelin' worse by the minute.'

Cassandra touched Bridget's forehead. It was fiercely hot and clammy. 'What do you think is the matter?' she asked helplessly.

Bridget was trying to control a violent fit of shivering. 'I—daresay 'tis no more than a touch of grippe. No doubt it was foolish of me to dunk my head in the river. If I can but get warm, I'm sure I shall sweat out the fever.'

Cassandra covered her with two of the pelts, and watched her with anxiety and dismay. But as the afternoon wore on Bridget's condition became alarmingly worse, and when she began to utter deliriously, Cassandra decided that she had no other course but to make their presence known to Gwylfa Jones.

His sloe-black eyes narrowed when he saw her appear from around the side of the lumbering wagon. He did not recognise her immediately; when he did so he uttered something in Welsh which could only have been a heartfelt oath.

Swiftly, Cassandra explained the situation to him. 'Which would be the quickest,' she asked in conclusion, 'to return to Ulundi, or press on to the British lines?'

He looked at her without expression. 'Neither.'

'What do you mean—neither?'

'I mean that I will not return to Ulundi. That is a gamble I do not choose to take. And I cannot press on to the British lines, even if I wanted to. I do not know where they are.'

'What—what do you mean? They couldn't have advanced very far since you left with the scouting party——'

'There was never a scouting party. I thought matters over, do you see, and it seemed to me that Lord Chelmsford would get his glorious victory without any sacrifices from me.' Jones smiled faintly. 'So I deserted, you understand. And since I do not choose to be shot, I must keep out of range of the British army.'

Cassandra blinked at him. 'But—where are we bound for, in that case?'

'*I* am bound for a place called Rorke's Drift,' he said, laying significant stress on the personal pronoun, 'and from there to the diamond mines of Kimberley to seek my fortune.'

At Ulundi, the disappearance of the two white girls was discovered by Esara at midmorning, and she made haste to inform Saul Parnell. He guessed at once what had happened, and cursed himself for having allowed Cassandra to trick him.

The anger gave way to anxiety. There was nothing he could put a finger on, but instinct warned him that the girls would not be safe with Gwylfa Jones.

He hurried to seek permission from the King to go after the girls. But Cetewayo stubbornly refused, seeing no reason to encumber himself with them again now that they had fortuitously been taken off his hands.

It was not until the following morning, after he had been racking his brains during a sleepless night, that Parnell perceived an argument which might well sway the King.

'The girl has your personal emblem of protection in her possession, Majesty. Think how that could be used against you by spies in the event of war!'

'War will be averted,' the King returned, but he looked thoughtful. 'Very well,' he gave in, 'go after them.'

Saul Parnell delayed only for as long as it took to have his horse saddled. He struck out towards the Lower

Drift of the Tugela River, where Gwylfa Jones had indicated his battalion was encamped with the British column. His horse could cover in a few hours a distance which would have taken a span of oxen all night, but there was no sign of a vehicle on the horizon, and neither could he find the tracks and spoor which would have proclaimed the recent passage of an ox-wagon.

His eyes narrowing against the fierce sun, he rode on. He had not yet reached the Tugela River, which formed the border between Natal and Zululand, when he perceived what was clearly a vanguard of British troops advancing towards him, His mouth tightened with impotent rage. There were still three days to go before the ultimatum expired, and already the British had, with unbelievable cynicism, invaded Zululand.

He reined in and awaited the approach of the British commanding officer and his following. Without dismounting, he asked—'Are you with the Twenty-fourth Regiment?'

'No, my man, we are not.' The British officer gave him a narrow-eyed look. 'I do not need to ask your identity. You are the man they call the Blue-Eyed Induna.'

'I am looking for a soldier, an infantryman attached to the Twenty-fourth. He had been released by King Cetewayo, after having been captured by Zulus, and was making his way by ox-wagon back to his battalion. He—may have left, quite inadvertently, with something which does not belong to him.'

The officer scratched his chin. 'If he was heading for his battalion, he would not have come this way. The Twenty-fourth are encamped at——' He stopped, and smiled thinly. 'I almost forgot that you are not one of us.'

Saul merely looked at him. 'You will not tell me where the Twenty-fourth are encamped?'

'No.' The officer hesitated. 'Look, you are as British as I am. You could be invaluable to our side, with your specialised knowledge of the Zulus. Join us, and you would be given a commission——'

When Parnell retained an impassive silence, the officer went on, 'I'm bound to tell you that I shall have to report on our meeting, and on the proposition which has been put to you.'

'Report away,' Saul recommended.

The officer's mouth tightened. 'You don't seem to realise what that means. You are refusing my offer?'

'I am.'

'Very well. I shall give you a sporting chance this time, for you were after all born British and a gentleman, even if you have chosen to go native. But I must warn you that the order will be given hereafter to treat you as a traitor and a spy. If you fall into British hands in the future, you will be shot.'

Without replying, Saul Parnell jerked his horse's head about and galloped away in the direction from which he had come. His brain was working furiously. His overriding impulse was to track the spoor of Gwylfa Jones, for things were not ringing true and he was more desperately anxious for the two girls than ever before. But cold duty told him that he must first return to Ulundi, and break the news to Cetewayo that Zululand had been invaded. Duty won.

The King was incredulous and baffled at first, and then bitter at what he regarded as the perfidious behaviour of the British. He decided to call an urgent meeting of the *i-bandla*.

Parnell drummed his fingers against his knees. 'May I be excused from attending the *i-bandla*, Majesty? I wish to lose no time in searching for the girls——'

'You would choose to be absent at such a critical occasion?' The King gave him a sharp, thoughtful look.

Saul shrugged. 'I would be more usefully employed, going after the girls. The more I think of it, the less I trust the Welsh soldier——'

'You will remain at Ulundi,' Cetewayo said shortly. He motioned to one of his bodyguards to announce a meeting of the *i-bandla*.

To Parnell's perplexed astonishment, the King sent a message to him, a short while later, informing him that he was to be excluded from the meeting of the *i-bandla*, but that he was not to leave the *kraal*. Saul watched from a distance as his fellow Indunas gathered to discuss the crisis.

After the meeting, the King ordered Saul to attend him once more. Cetewayo sat in silence for a while, before he said, 'You wish to leave Ulundi.'

'To go after the Welshman and the girls—yes, Majesty.'

'There would be nothing to stop you from joining the British impis afterwards,' the King stated flatly.

'I have no intention of doing so——'

'You have much knowledge,' Cetewayo went on, as if he hadn't spoken, 'which would be useful to the British.'

'Have I ever given you cause to doubt my loyalty, Majesty?' Saul demanded.

'You refused to marry Esara,' the King said obscurely, 'even though I gave you the Royal permission, and her father desired it. You did not, perhaps, wish to ally yourself too closely with my people.'

'That was not my——'

'You may leave my presence now,' the King interrupted dismissively, 'and remain in the *kraal* until I send for you once more.'

Saul could understand the King's reaction. Cetewayo was bewildered and deeply wounded by the, to him, unexpected invasion of the British. If the British could behave like this towards an erstwhile friend, the King must be reasoning, then why should the Blue-Eyed Induna not display similar treachery? And of course, it was quite true that Saul possessed intimate knowledge about the Zulus which would be of inestimable value to the British in the coming war.

Saul kicked his heels, waiting for the King to summon him once more, marshalling his arguments to convince Cetewayo of his loyalty. And at the same time he tried not to allow his imagination to run riot as he thought of Cassandra and Bridget in Gwylfa Jones's dubious custody.

Cetewayo did not, however, send for his Blue-Eyed Induna. Saul watched from a distance as regimental bulls were driven into the barracks, a certain prelude to military action. The animals would be ceremonially slaughtered, their flesh shared out among the warriors, and their blood mixed with herbs by the witch doctors in a war potion.

That night Saul sat alone in his hut, and listened to the martial chanting of the warriors, to their repeated yells of *'Nkosi yama Kosi!'* as they saluted their King.

A shadow fell across the doorway. Esara sidled furtively into the hut, and knelt before him. 'Induna,' she said gravely, 'I come to warn you that there is to be a smelling-out tonight.'

Parnell stiffened. The smelling-out of witches was an old tribal custom usually with two aims—to placate the gods, and to rid the tribe simultaneously of a dangerous or uncongenial presence. The 'witch' to be smelt out was almost always pre-selected, and there was only one conclusion to the ceremony. The 'witch' faced impalement on a wooden stake.

So that was how Cetewayo meant to deal with his Blue-Eyed Induna, who had now become a danger to him as well as a hateful reminder of the treachery of the

British.

'You must leave at once, Induna,' Esara urged. 'I have saddled your horse, and hidden him beyond the stake-and-wattle fence.'

He cupped her face briefly in his hand. 'Yes. Thank you.'

Tears shone in her eyes. '*Hamba gahle, Induna*,' she whispered. 'Go well.'

'*Sala gahle*, Esara,' he responded quietly. 'Stay well.'

As he moved cautiously among the huts, towards the outer fence surrounding Ulundi, Saul remembered how he had once faced the fact that he would soon have to play the traitor towards one side or the other.

It had never occurred to him that he might become a fugitive from both sides, his life in danger from Briton and Zulu alike.

CHAPTER
SIX

GWYLFA JONES had jumped from the driver's seat and had crawled beneath the canopy of the wagon where Bridget was lying, covered in pelts and muttering incoherently in her fever.

'Many of the troops suffered a similar kind of ague as we marched towards Zululand,' he told Cassandra. 'It struck without warning, but lasted only a day or two. If that is what she is suffering from, then it is not serious.'

'You can't be certain,' Cassandra argued. 'It could be anything. She needs medicine—preferably European medicine, but failing that some herbal potion of the Zulus. Since you can't take us to the British lines, you must return us to Ulundi——'

'No.'

'But you must! I demand that you take us without delay——'

His eyebrows rose. In that slow, sing-song but utterly inexorable voice of his, he said, 'You are in no position to demand anything, Miss. You are not on this wagon by my invitation I have no responsibility towards either of you.'

She glared at him in impotent fury. 'Look, I can understand why you won't take us to the British lines They would shoot you for the miserable deserter you are. But we are not very far from Ulundi, and you have nothing to fear by returning us there——'

The sloe-black eyes looked cynically amused. 'No? Even if you did not tell your Zulu friends that I have deserted, they would soon guess it for themselves if I returned. They would know that I could not have set out last night for the direction in which I had told them the British were encamped. They would guess that I had intended to steal their king's pelts. I do not think they would be very pleased to know I had made fools of them, and that they had put on that fearsome display of warriors for nothing. No, Miss, I will not take you back to Ulundi.'

'But—but surely you can't mean to carry us off, willy-nilly, to Kimberley with you?'

'No, indeed. That would not do at all. It will be necessary for me to take on a new identity, do you see, if I am to keep out of the hands of the British Army. And how could I do that, encumbered with two females who would betray me at the earliest opportunity?'

Cassandra moistened her lips. 'If you refuse to return us to Ulundi, and you won't take us to Kimberley with you, then that means you—that you intend abandoning us . . .'

He said unemotionally—'I have no choice, Miss.'

'But you *can't* abandon us! It would be monstrous!'

'It's a hard old life, Miss, and we must each look out for ourselves, isn't it.'

'You might just as well take your gun,' Cassandra cried, 'and shoot both of us dead right now!'

'There's dramatic, Miss,' Jones reproved phlegmatically. 'We are not very far from Ulundi, as you said. You could quite easily walk back to the *kraal*, following the tracks we have left behind us. It should not take you more than a day and a half.'

'How do you expect Bridget to walk in her condition?' Cassandra demanded angrily.

He hesitated, and then shrugged. 'If I am right, and she is suffering from the same ague which struck down so many of the troops, she will be feeling fit as a fiddle again quite soon.'

He jumped from the wagon. Defeatedly, Cassandra mopped Bridget's hot forehead and cursed the fates which had conspired to bring them to this hopeless and frightening situation.

Gwylfa Jones had been reconnoitring the surroundings in which they had come to a halt, and he returned to the wagon. 'I have found a spot where you will be quite snug, Miss.'

Cassandra merely looked at him in contempt. He began to dismantle the canvas canopy from the wagon, talking as he worked.

'You would not have liked it at Kimberley, Miss Rough, it is—or so they say. Attracts the scum of the earth. Yes, Miss, I know what you are thinking, and it's entitled to your opinion you are.'

He had detached the canopy from the wagon, and now he began to manhandle it down a slope towards a straggly line of stunted bushes. He returned to the wagon, taking from it armfuls of animal pelts and provisions.

'There you are, Miss,' he addressed Cassandra, when he returned from his final trip. 'I have set up the canopy close to a stream, so you will have all the water you need. I am leaving you almost all the food the Zulus presented to me. And your maid will be far more comfortable lying on the animal pelts under the canopy than she ever was on the jolting wagon. In a day or two, when she has recovered, you could walk back to Ulundi.'

'Do you expect me to thank you?' Cassandra cried with angry scorn. 'Of all the despicable things you have done, this is the very worst! Leaving us here, with poor Bridget perhaps mortally ill——'

'If that is so, Miss,' he interposed bluntly, 'then it will not matter very much from her point of view whether she is to die on a jolting wagon somewhere on the road to Kimberley, or right here.'

'You heartless brute! You can talk so calmly of Bridget dying!'

'People are dying all the time, Miss.' There was a stark edge to his voice now. 'Death is no stranger to me, so why should I not be calm about it?'

Panic filled Cassandra as she glimpsed the horrifying possibilities facing her, alone and vulnerable and responsible for her sick maid.

'You are utterly inhuman!' she told Jones. 'Anything could happen to us, alone out here! How am I to defend the two of us against wild animals, for instance?'

'There is no dangerous big game left in these parts.' His voice had turned rough, as if he were fighting against some faint stirring of conscience about what he proposed to do. 'The most you need fear is disturbing a snake. And I shall find a stout stick for you with which to arm yourself.'

'If you weren't thinking only of your own skin, you could have taken us to safety——'

For the first time since she had met him, Cassandra saw passion flickering in those flat black eyes of his. 'Why do the likes of you always expect sacrifices from the likes of me, Miss? Why should *my* life be worth so much less than yours?'

He did not wait for her reaction, but gathered Bridget in his arms, and jumped from the wagon. Cassandra had no alternative but to follow him down the slope to where he had set up the canvas canopy.

As he crawled through the flap with Bridget, and attempted to lay her down on the animal pelts which he had spread on the ground, the maid clung to him and muttered in distress.

'I've lost the ewe, Rory . . . . I've not the—strength in me at all—for climbin' the hills. Another blizzard the night—and she'll die for sure—and her with her lambin' not far off . . .'

Cassandra, who had listened to Bridget's delirious utterances before, knew that she was reliving her childhood and early youth on an Irish small-holding among the mountains. Surprisingly, Gwylfa Jones did not ignore the girl's ravings; instead, he said in a soothing voice, 'I have gathered in the ewe all right and tight, *cariad.*'

Bridget's plain, pinched features were momentarily transformed by a look of joy and contentment. 'Rory, I'm thinkin'—'twas the saints themselves sent you . . .' Her voice turned anxious. '*You'll* not leave me too?'

Cassandra watched his hand lifting slowly towards Bridget's head. There was something still and thoughtful and almost tender about him as he smoothed the spiky ginger hair from the girl's forehead.

Then, abruptly, he loosened the grip she still had upon him. 'I am not your Rory,' he told her in a hard voice. Ignoring the tears which had begun to well from her eyes, he deposited her upon the pelts and turned to Cassandra.

'You will be snug enough here until you can walk to Ulundi. Follow the trail where the wagon wheels flattened the grass, and you will not get lost. Goodbye, Miss.'

Cassandra made no reply. A little later she listened dully as he cracked the whip over the oxen, and the wagon began to trundle on again.

Cassandra made Bridget as comfortable as she could, offering her frequent drinks of water, spongeing her hot face and keeping her covered with the animal pelts. During one of her lucid spells, Bridget allowed Cassandra to bully her into eating a little cornbread. The fact that she had broken her fast encouraged Cassandra; perhaps Bridget was on the mend, and they could soon begin to walk back to Ulundi.

But after a comfortless night spent under the canopy, Bridget's fever was as high as ever. And now it was useless to try and persuade her to swallow broiled meat or cornbread; what she needed was nourishing gruels or broth. The longer she went without food, the less strength she would have for fighting the fever.

As the day wore on, fears threaded through Cassandra's brain, threatening to overwhelm her. When the abrupt African darkness fell for the second time since Jones had left them there, total despair engulfed her, until a sudden thought occurred to her, bringing dizzying relief.

Saul Parnell would come after them! Of course he would! He would have set out to look for them as soon as it was discovered that she and Bridget had disappeared from Ulundi. By now, he must have realised that Gwylfa Jones had not taken the direction expected of him, and Parnell was probably scouring the landscape, looking for their wagon tracks. All she had to do was to keep her head, and sooner or later he would find them .

A shattering clap of thunder cut through her thoughts. She crawled to the flap of the canopy, peering outside. A fat dark cloud rolled ponderously across the moon, and was followed by another. It struck Cassandra that she had never experienced rain in Zulu land before

When it came, the rain began innocently enough, with large, lazy drops thudding on the canvas roof of the canopy and filling the air with the not unpleasant smell of wet soil. But without warning the sky seemed to split asunder with a savage blaze of lightning. At the same moment as the thunder rolled across the veld, a barrage of rain came down.

Cassandra, accustomed to the gentle, insistent drizzles in London, had never experienced anything like this deluge before. It drove underneath the canvas canopy, soaking the animal pelts, and she tried frantically to keep Bridget dry and warm somehow.

It was not until some while later that she realised how far-reaching the results of the downpour would be. The savage rain would have obliterated all signs of the wagon's trail. Not only would Saul Parnell be unable to follow its tracks in search of them, but even if and when Bridget did recover, they would not be able to find their way back to Ulundi. They would be hopelessly lost.

The sudden storm had forced Saul to pause in his flight from Ulundi, and to seek shelter in a cave-like fissure cut into the gorge. As he waited for the fury of the rain to abate, he mused bleakly upon his situation.

Cetewayo could not afford to turn a blind eye to the escape of his Blue-Eyed Induna. For one thing, Saul possessed too much knowledge which would be dangerous to the Zulus if he were to ally himself with the British. But even more important, the King would lose face with his people if he did not have Saul hunted to death.

By now, Saul knew quite well, his escape would have been reported to the King. He could only hope that Esara's part in it would not become known. Cetewayo would have lost no time in sending messengers to all the other *kraals* scattered throughout Zululand, and by midday tomorrow everyone in Cetewayo's kingdom would know that the Blue-Eyed Induna was a wanted fugitive. There would be no refuge for him anywhere.

Cursing the downpour, he acknowledged to himself that he would have to cover as much ground as possible during the hours of darkness, and hide out during the day. Even when he had left Zululand and crossed the border into Natal he would not be safe, for then he would risk being arrested as a spy and a traitor against the British.

The one possible solution to the dilemma—that of offering his services to the British, and seeking sanctuary among their lines—he discarded without even considering it. Even though he would never again have a place among them, he could not betray his adopted people.

He sighed heavily. His first necessity was to leave Zululand as swiftly and stealthily as possible. He would make his way towards Rorke's Drift, and cross the Buffalo River into Natal. And then he would somehow have to lose himself without trace.

As soon as the fury of the storm abated a little, he mounted his horse, and sped on towards the direction of Rorke's Drift. Dawn broke with flamboyant streaks of rose along the horizon, reminding him irrelevantly of the absurdly frivolous French bonnet which Cassandra had worn the first time he laid eyes upon her.

He would have preferred not to have been reminded of Cassandra Hudson, for he would never see her again. He had abandoned the search for her and Bridget; they would be far safer with Gwylfa Jones than they could ever be with himself, now.

He thrust the thought of Cassandra away. He would have to water his horse soon, and then find somewhere to lie low during the daylight hours. He knew of a stream a short distance away, and a *donga* or gully not far from it which was so overgrown with scrub and thorn that it was virtually undetectable to the uninitiated eye. The *donga* would provide both shelter for him and grazing for his horse.

He was picking his way towards the line of stunted trees which denoted the existence of a stream when movement through the branches caught his eye. He dismounted and crept stealthily forward.

With utter amazement, he discerned the slight figure of a European youth dressed in homespun breeches and shirt, standing by the stream with his back turned to Parnell. The youth pulled the shirt over his head and then, kneeling beside the stream, began to splash water over his arms.

Saul's frown deepened. There was something incongruous about the appearance and manner of the youth. Besides, where could he have come from? The nearest white mission was at Rorke's Drift.

Abandoning caution, Saul strode towards the stream. And it was only when his shadow fell across the water, and she whirled around in terror, that he recognised Cassandra.

Several swift reactions surged through Cassandra. Instinctive fright at first, then amazement at the sight of Parnell, followed by a mixture of tangled emotions in which joyous relief was only an incidental part. Impulsively, she ran to him, flinging her arms about him.

'Oh, thank God, thank God! I might have known you would find us! My dear Blue-Eyed Induna . . .'

Automatically, his fingers moved upon the silky flesh of her shoulders. She lifted her face to his, her eyes wide with the wonder of her sudden discovery, her full mouth yielding.

He caught her to him with a harsh intake of breath. There was a kind of savage tenderness in the way he held her against him, his hands moving unsteadily upon her bare flesh. And yet he did not kiss her, even though she deliberately offered him her lips once more. A tremor passed through his body. He pushed her away, and said coldly, 'Put your shirt on. You look ridiculous; neither one sex nor the other.'

Colour washed into her cheeks. She grabbed the shirt and pulled it over her head, then faced Parnell again. 'I don't know how you are to take us back to Ulundi, with only one horse between us——'

'I haven't any intention of taking you back to Ulundi.' He frowned at her. 'What do you mean? Where are the wagon and oxen?'

'Jones abandoned us, and drove to Rorke's Drift.' She told him the story from the beginning, and concluded, 'Bridget is no better this morning, and I dare say getting wet during last night's storm won't improve her condition.' Cassandra's voice shook slightly. 'Even if—if you mean to wash your hands of me, as you seem to be implying, won't you—at least take Bridget back to Ulundi with you?'

He said bleakly, 'I can't go back to Ulundi. I had to flee for my life. And since I'm under sentence of death, Cassandra, anyone in my company would be summarily executed by the Zulus too if they find me.'

She stared at him, hardly taking in the fact that the British had invaded Zululand as he recounted what had happened. It seemed unbelievable that King Cetewayo should have turned on his Blue-Eyed Induna.

'Take me to Bridget now,' Saul concluded, 'and I'll see what I can do for her.'

The little maid's fever was still dangerously high, and she was barely conscious. Saul frowned as he stared at the sodden canvas canopy which was steaming in the early morning heat, and at the damp pelts upon which she was lying.

'We must bring her temperature down,' he said, 'but we can't do anything about that until we have a change of dry clothing for her, and dry coverings with which to keep her warm. I'm going to move her to a place I know of, Cassandra. In the meantime, spread out these pelts to dry in the sun.'

A short while later he came back to Cassandra. The far end of the *donga* to which he led her formed a shallow cave, and in this he had laid Bridget down.

'She has eaten virtually nothing since we left Ulundi,' Cassandra said worriedly.

Saul nodded, and examined the provisions which Esara had hastily packed for him the night before. Among it was a hide container full of the sweet–sour beer which the Zulu women brewed from ground mealiemeal.

'It's really not much more than fermented gruel,' Saul explained, 'and can only do her good.'

But Bridget gagged on the unfamiliar fermented taste, and Saul said reflectively, 'What she needs is some nourishing broth. Did I see a cooking pot under the canopy?'

'Yes. Jones was generous enough to leave us one, even though we had no hope of obtaining anything to cook in it.'

Saul nodded, thankful that he had grabbed his hunting spear before leaving Ulundi. A gunshot would have been a foolhardy risk under the circumstances. Armed with the spear, he left the *donga*, and it was not very long afterwards that he returned with the carcass of a young deer. By the time that had been skinned and cut up, and part of it was simmering on the fire which Saul had built, he pronounced that it would be safe, now, to reduce Bridget's temperature.

To Cassandra's horror, he insisted that they undress Bridget, and immerse her repeatedly in the cold water of the stream. Cassandra protested, and Bridget herself moaned faintly each time she was subjected to this treatment.

'She'll die of pneumonia!' Cassandra gasped.

'No, she won't. There, that's enough, I think. Let's rub her dry, now, and dress her warmly.'

Bridget did seem to have benefited from such drastic treatment, for her temperature had dropped, and she was able to drink a considerable amount of the broth. At sunset she was inside the cave, wrapped in dry pelts, and appeared to be sleeping normally.

Cassandra and Saul sat by the fire, broiling pieces of deer meat for their own supper.

'There's sufficient broth left for Bridget for tomorrow,' he broke the silence. 'By the time she has finished that, she ought to be able to eat solid food again, and you seem to be well supplied with that.'

Cassandra caught her lower lip between her teeth 'You—sound as if you won't be here tomorrow.'

He nodded. 'I'm leaving as soon as it's completely dark.'

'No!' she cried involuntarily.

'My dear girl, if you're feeling safer because I'm here, that is a dangerous illusion.' There was a bleak note in his voice. 'I'm like a—like a plague-carrying animal. I bring the threat of violent death to anyone I associate with while I'm in Zululand. The greatest service I could do you is to remove myself from your presence.'

'You must stay at least for tonight,' she said desperately. 'You must promise not to leave until we know whether Bridget will recover or not.'

He sighed. 'If I have not succeeded in bringing Bridget's temperature down by what I did today, then there is nothing more I *can* do There would be no point in my staying.'

'I need you,' Cassandra said jerkily. 'I—love—you . . .'

He was utterly still for an instant. Then his head came up, and in the firelight his eyes were blue and cold and hard. 'You are talking childish rubbish,' he said frostily.

Her mouth quivered, and she turned her face away. She heard him go on, his words falling like cruel whip-lashes upon her spirit.

'You'll find your cousin Martin when all this is over. You'll marry him, and wear fancy bonnets, and teach poor heathen children that cats in England sit on mats. That is what you have come out here for. Don't lose sight of reality in your absurd flights of fancy.'

He rose abruptly, and walked away, unable to go on witnessing the shock and pain in her eyes. Hadn't she taken in anything he had been telling her? he wondered angrily. Did she realise that he was destined to be a hunted man for the rest of his life? The memory of the British Army was long and vengeful; even if the war in Zululand lasted no more than a week, he would still remain branded as a traitor and a spy, liable to be tried and shot. If there was any future for him at all, it lay in some half-world like the diamond mines of Kimberley, where almost every adventurer had a secret past and no one asked questions. Only among other fugitives, among remittance men and human flotsam, would he be safe from now on.

Wearily, he passed a hand across his face. He would fight the overwhelming impulse to retract his brutish words to her. Let her remember him as the callous lout who had flung her declaration of love back at her so cruelly, and let her marry her pious cousin.

But when it came to it, he could not deny himself the dubious comfort of postponing his departure, and spending a few more hours with her. When he returned to the fire, he said shortly,

'I'll stay here tonight, since you're anxious about Bridget. But tomorrow evening I'm riding for Rorke's Drift. I'm bound to overtake Gwylfa Jones on the way; by the time I've finished with him he'll beg to be allowed to come back for you and take you to Rorke's Drift. You'll be safe there at the Swedish Mission.'

Cassandra did not trust herself to answer, but merely nodded. She moved away from the fire, and lay down beside Bridget and tried to sleep. But she was only too painfully aware that Saul had settled himself for the night near the entrance of the cave and that he, too, was only pretending to be asleep.

But towards dawn exhaustion must have overcome him, for she could tell by his rhythmic breathing that now he really was asleep. At last she could seek relief from the claustrophobic despair which had enveloped her all night. She rose quietly and stole out of the cave, intent only on finding a quiet, lonely spot where she could give way to tears.

She had not strayed far from the *donga* when she heard a frantic voice calling in the morning air.

'Miss! Miss Hudson! Bridget! *Miss*!'

She blinked incredulously. It was Gwylfa Jones's voice. But he should be on his way to Rorke's Drift—and where were the wagon and the oxen?

She hurried towards the spot where he had set up the canvas canopy for them. He saw her, and came hurrying to meet her.

'What are you doing here?' Cassandra demanded breathlessly.

'I came back, see.' There was something like sheepish defiance in his glance. 'But not because of you, mind. I came back because of Bridget. I thought of her, in all that rain. How is she, Miss? Where is she?'

'She's safely asleep. Her fever seems to have broken.' Cassandra glanced about her. 'What have you done with the wagon and oxen?'

'Well, now . . .' He rubbed his hand along his jaw. 'I no longer have them, do you see.'

'Why not?' Cassandra asked sharply. 'What happened to them?'

'It was this way, Miss. I had turned back for you, when I gradually realised that I was being stalked by two armed warriors. Playing with me, they were—following me through the long grass with their spears, not trying to stop me. But perhaps they were keeping out of range of my gun, not knowing that it was useless. The Zulus at Ulundi had taken my bullets.

'Fair rattled me, it did, Miss. When darkness fell I seized my chance. I quietly abandoned the wagon and the oxen, and came on here on foot. I reckoned the warriors must have had their eye on the oxen, and I was right for there has been no sign of them since——'

With uncanny timing, almost as if it were a tableau unfolding upon a stage, Jones's last words coincided with a rustling movement in the scrub, and the next instant two warriors sprang towards them, their spears raised, a frightening yell upon their lips.

Cassandra stood transfixed with terror. One of the spears was almost touching her throat, while another was poised a fraction of an inch from Gwylfa Jones's heart. The warrior menacing him was intoning something in an awesome voice, as if he were solemnly pronouncing a sentence of death upon them. Cassandra was certain that she was about to die.

Saul Parnell was certain too. He had been roused by Gwylfa Jones's call, and had followed Cassandra from the cave. The scrubby trees hid him from view of the Zulus, but he had seen and heard enough to know that Cassandra was about to die with Jones. The warriors had learnt all about the Welsh soldier by bush telegraph; they knew that he must have intended to steal the King's gift of pelts. And they believed Cassandra to be his accomplice.

The warrior finished his accusation. At that instant Saul stepped out of the cover of the trees.

'*Ni ngama qawu*!' he called a salutation to the Zulus.

'*Hé*!' The spears were lowered slightly as they turned to study Saul. They obviously did not know him by sight.

Deliberately, he addressed them once more in their own tongue, ordering them, as Cetewayo's Blue-Eyed Induna, to lay down their spears.

Realisation dawned on their faces. One of them exclaimed something and they advanced towards Saul, ignoring Cassandra and Jones now. They had never seen him before, but they clearly knew that the Blue-Eyed Induna was under sentence of death.

He paused only long enough to shout, 'Get to Rorke's Drift somehow! Take my horse!' Then he was zig-zagging through the long grass, the warriors in purposeful pursuit and rapidly gaining on him.

He could not possibly hope to escape them, Cassandra thought dully. They had only to get close enough to him to throw their murderous spears. She would never see him again, and she would have to live with the knowledge that he had deliberately revealed his identity to the warriors in order to save her from death.

If that was a declaration of love, it would have to be enough for the rest of her life. She would have nothing else with which to comfort herself.

CHAPTER
SEVEN

SAUL and his pursuers had been swallowed up by the long grass, only the turbulent waves along its surface betraying the desperate and dangerous activity taking place within its cover. Cassandra ran towards an enormous anthill and clambered to the top, from which she had a clearer view of them.

Saul seemed to be deliberately reserving his strength and remaining just out of reach of the two Zulus, as if to tantalise them. They, for their part, made no attempt to bring him down with their throwing spears, and suddenly she realised that they would wish to deliver him alive to Cetewayo. They would only throw their spears as a last resort, if they could see no possibility of overtaking him.

But he could not go on running indefinitely. The most he was probably hoping for was to gain time, so that Cassandra, Bridget and Gwylfa Jones would be able to get away safely.

Cassandra's first despairing, fatalistic mood was giving way to one of rebellion. There had to be some means of saving Saul from the Zulus ...

She ran back to Gwylfa Jones, who was looking as stolidly enigmatic as if no drama had just taken place.

'You must go after them!' she said breathlessly. 'You must help Saul——'

'And how would I do that, Miss?' he demanded in a humouring tone. 'Of what use would I be against their spears, with no weapon of my own? If I'd had bullets for my gun, perhaps——'

'Gun!' Cassandra echoed. 'Saul had a rifle! He must have left it in the *donga* when he heard you calling to me. He had no reason to suppose that he might need it .   '

'He was wearing his bandolier,' Gwylfa Jones mused. 'Force of habit, of course. A pity that.' He brightened. 'But there is sure to be a round of bullets in his gun. We will doubtless have need of those bullets before we reach Rorke's Drift.'

Jones was not even fleetingly entertaining the idea of helping Saul. For some quixotic reason he felt concern for Bridget, but there his compassion ended. It would be worse than useless to plead with him, Cassandra knew; it would be a dangerous waste of time.

She began to walk rapidly towards the *donga*, with Jones following. But as if her intentions had somehow communicated themselves to him, he began to lengthen his stride, and Cassandra was forced to break into a run. She reached the spot where Saul had left his rifle and other belongings, a split second before Jones did so. With trembling hands she levelled the gun at him.

'If you try to grab it, I'll shoot you,' she warned.

'Now Miss, it's foolish you're being. You know nothing about guns——'

'I know how to release the safety catch and pull the trigger!'

'You wouldn't shoot me, Miss. Not a gently-reared young lady like yourself.' He was confidently advancing towards her.

'Let me assure you,' Cassandra told him with cold menace, 'that I won't have the slightest hesitation in wasting one of the bullets on you if I have to. I'm going after Saul, to help him, and you won't stop me!'

Jones had halted his advance. 'How could you help him, Miss?' he argued. 'Do you imagine the Zulus would obligingly stand still while you shoot them in the back, even supposing you caught up with them in time?'

'I don't know how I'll help him, but something will surely occur to me. And I'll catch up with them, for I mean to take Saul's horse.'

Jones whistled soundlessly. 'You and the horse would make a fine target for the Zulus' spears!'

'That can't be helped. I'll need the horse. Besides,' Cassandra added grimly, 'I've no doubt at all that if I left the beast behind, I'd return to find that you'd disappeared with it and the bulk of our supplies. Now, would you please saddle the horse for me?'

Jones looked as if he meant to refuse, then changed his mind with a shrug and picked up the saddle. Cassandra did not relax her vigilance. She could not imagine Gwylfa Jones, with his instinct for self-preservation, lightly risking two such valuable commodities as the horse and the gun falling into Zulu hands, and she suspected a last-minute trick.

But he seemed resigned as he handed the bridle to her. When he offered to help her into the saddle she smiled sardonically and refused.

'Please look after Bridget for me. When she awakens, heat some of the broth in the cooking pot for her.'

With the rifle over her shoulder, she led the horse to the nearest anthill. Gwylfa Jones followed slowly, watching her, but made no attempt to stop her. She climbed the anthill, balanced the rifle against the pommel and heaved herself on to the animal's back.

As soon as her weight pressed down upon the horse she knew that Jones had tricked her after all. He must have placed a bouquet of the ferocious wait-a-minute thorns which grew in such abundance in the *donga* beneath the saddle, for the horse was frenziedly trying to rid itself of Cassandra. She clung on with blind single-mindedness, and the maddened horse bolted, bucking and rearing. Jones came running towards them, but horse and rider flashed by him.

Somehow, Cassandra succeeded in placing her feet in the stirrups so that she could raise her weight from the saddle. The horse was only marginally appeased, to the extent that it now accepted the trail along which Cassandra steered it—the track of flattened grass which had been left by Saul and his pursuers.

Far too soon, and long before she was ready for it, Cassandra could see the three running figures ahead. They were skirting the edge of a line of trees which usually denoted the existence of a river or stream. There was no time to plan anything. She reached for the rifle, and in doing so she had to place her full weight on the saddle once more. The horse, enraged by this gratuitous assault, shot forward with what sounded like a high-pitched snarl.

The next minutes were to be for ever afterwards jumbled chaotically in Cassandra's mind. The Zulus stopped in their tracks, and turned A spear whistled through the air, nicking the horse's ear before falling to the ground. Gunshots cracked out, even though Cassandra had made no conscious decision to pull the trigger. Then she was flying through the air as the horse at last succeeded in ridding itself of her. She was concussed and unconscious for a while, and when she opened her eyes and struggled upright Saul was engaged in a grim and silent battle with one of the Zulus. The other was lying some distance away, spread-eagled face down, and already two vultures were wheeling high overhead.

Cassandra's gaze went fearfully to the struggle which was taking place close by her. Saul and the Zulu were locked in desperate combat and Saul appeared destined to get the worst of it. He was on his back, with the Zulu straddled across him, and the latter's assegai poised over his heart. Saul's hand was clamped across the Zulu's wrist as he struggled for possession of the assegai.

Wildly and sickly, Cassandra looked about her for the rifle, but it had been dropped somewhere in the long grass and she could not find it. She was wondering frantically what else she could possibly use as a weapon to help Saul when she heard a grunt, and she spun around. The Zulu lay in a curious crouching position, impaled on his own assegai, and Saul was struggling to his feet.

Cassandra ran towards him. 'Oh, thank God, thank God you're safe!' she breathed, clutching his arm.

He hurled her away from him with one ferocious movement, so that she staggered and almost fell. He stalked away, towards the belt of trees. After a stunned moment Cassandra followed him. He was leaning against one of the trees with his head in his hands.

Tentatively, Cassandra said, 'I—know that you're upset because two Zulus are dead, and you looked upon them as your people. But—but if we hadn't killed them, they would have killed you ...'

He removed his hands from his face and gave her a bleak look. '*We* did not kill them, Cassandra. You don't share my guilt. I killed both of them. All you achieved was to put a bullet in the back of my shoulder.'

He drew his hand across his right shoulder-blade as he spoke, and when he held it out to her she saw that it was stained with blood. She looked at him with huge, shocked eyes, and momentarily the world seemed to spin around her.

'Don't treat me to a fit of the vapours!' she heard him say harshly, from what seemed a long way away. 'There isn't time. Those bodies will have to be protected against vultures, but first you'll have to dig out the bullet you've put into me.'

His astringent voice banished the fainting spell which had threatened to overcome her. She swallowed hard. 'I'm sorry I shot you. But—you might at least give me credit for *something*. I created a diversion, made it possible for you to——'

'You made it *necessary* for me to kill.'

'I don't understand,' she said in a small voice. 'I don't really know what happened. The horse was running away with me——'

'I'll tell you what happened. After the horse had thrown you, the first Zulu was about to impale you to the ground with his throwing spear. I was forced to jump on him from behind and break his neck. The second Zulu wasted a few seconds in searching for the rifle, so I had time to brace myself before he came at me with his assegai.'

His gaze rested upon her, his blue eyes hard and unforgiving. 'If you hadn't interfered no one would have been hurt. I knew precisely what I was doing. Why couldn't you have minded your own damned business?'

Tears filled her eyes at the ferocity of his attack. The sight of them did not soften him. He said brusquely, 'Save your self-pity for later. There's a river beyond these trees; you'll need to clean up the wound before you dig for the bullet.'

Wordlessly, Cassandra followed him through the trees. The river was wide and turbulent after the recent rains, its brown water foaming across rocks and flattening the reeds which grew in the centre.

'Keep your eyes open for a white crocodile,' Saul said, something cruelly mocking in his voice, as he sat down on a rock by the water's edge and pulled his shirt over his head.

'A—*white* crocodile?' Cassandra faltered, intuitively aware that his reference to such an unlikely creature was meant, obscurely, to punish her further.

'A white crocodile is reputed to inhabit the river some way further up. Personally, I can't believe that an albino crocodile could have survived to adulthood without any of the normal camouflage, but several Zulus swear they've seen it, and they all have a superstitious dread of it.'

Saul's hard gaze met hers. 'That's where I was making for. I knew the two Zulus would not follow me into the river. I'd planned to dive in and swim underwater until I was out of range of their throwing spears.'

Cassandra was silent, completely numbed by the consequences of her own rash impulsiveness. Small wonder that Saul held her in such bitter contempt. Her interference had accomplished nothing but the needless death of two men and a bullet in his shoulder.

The bullet was not deeply lodged. After carefully washing the knife he had handed her, Cassandra gritted her teeth as she probed at it, loosening it from the surrounding tissue. Only a muffled groan escaped Saul, but when she had completed the operation his face was bloodless beneath the tan.

She plugged the wound with strips of lawn which she tore from the chemisette she wore beneath her homespun shirt. Then, without speaking, the two of them began to collect stones from the river with which to cover the bodies of the Zulus.

It was a gruelling task, and Saul was hampered by his painful wound. The afternoon sun was low in the sky by the time the dead Zulus had been decently covered with stones. Saul performed a curious and oddly moving little ceremony, commending their souls to their forefathers. As Cassandra listened to the clicking, sonorous Zulu words the enormity of what she had done weighed upon her like an enormous burden, and she turned aside.

'I'll take you back to the *donga* before I go my own

way,' she heard Saul say shortly. 'But first of all I want to search for the rifle and for my horse. There are wild figs growing by the river. You'd better eat some.'

She realised that she had not eaten all day, but she felt no hunger. She was consumed by a black tide of guilt and misery, and she welcomed the chance to give way to her feelings in private. Saul would have looked at her with contempt and called it self-pity. . . .

She found a spot some distance away where trees grew densely, and threw herself down on the grass. With her head cradled on her arms, she gave way to a storm of weeping. She had bargained on Saul's search occupying him for at least an hour, but within only a few minutes he was calling out to her in an impatient voice. She tried desperately to conquer her tears.

When he joined her she was sitting with her knees drawn up to her chin, her eyes shaded by her hand.

'I've found the rifle,' he said. 'There's no sign of my horse. There's just a chance that he might have gone back to the *donga*. If he hasn't, I'll have to give him up for lost.'

'I'm sorry,' Cassandra managed to say evenly, and then betrayed herself with a hiccuping sob.

He hesitated, and sank on to the ground beside her. 'Don't cry,' he said quietly. 'You acted with the best of intentions. You showed great courage and I shouldn't have attacked you so unmercifully.'

'Two men—have died—and there was no need . . .' she sobbed.

He sighed heavily. 'A great many more men will die before long, with even less need. That's a fact of war. Besides, how do we know that my original plan would have worked? Perhaps you did save my life. So stop punishing yourself.'

This time she could not control the dry sobs which shook her. He pulled her down beside him and held her, his hand moving over her stubby curls. At last she grew still and opened her eyes, looking full into his. She had caught him unawares, and the expression in his blue eyes was vulnerable and strangely tormented.

'Saul—kiss me—please?' she whispered.

He swore under his breath. 'Don't—goad me——'

She blinked before the raw emotion in his voice. Already he was drawing away from her, a bleak and distant look in his eyes now. Instinctively and without thought, she employed every feminine appeal which had until now lain dormant in her own passionate nature, curving her body against his, moving her hands gently along his side.

His eyes darkened. His fingers fumbled with the buttons of her homespun boy's shirt and she felt the warmth of his mouth on her shoulder and bare throat. As his lips moved upon hers, afterwards, she had an odd feeling as if she were falling through a dark and bottomless void. He filled her heart and her mind and her body, until she ceased to exist as a separate being.

When, at last, he moved away from her she said quietly, 'I do love you, you know. And it's not childish rubbish, or an absurd fantasy.'

He was silent for a moment, his eyes fixed upon some inner distant horizon from which he derived no pleasure. At last he said, 'You're forcing me to spell out what I hadn't been quite brutal enough to say to you last night. I don't love you.'

He saw the pain and disbelief in her eyes, and knew that he had to deliver the *coup de grâce* and kill stone-dead all hope and tenderness in her heart. His mouth was filled with a bitter taste of self-contempt for his own weakness and lack of self-control, but he allowed none of this to show.

'You're not the first pretty girl I've made love to,' he said lightly, 'and you certainly won't be the last. But as

for love. . . . There *is* someone—a woman in D'Urban;
a real, grown up woman who knows how to make a man
feel ten feet tall. Unfortunately she's married to someone else. And that is why I amuse myself with pretty
little girls.'

He saw Cassandra's face whiten, and noted with sick
satisfaction the passionate rage and bitter humiliation in
her eyes. She rose, and said in a stony voice, 'It's
getting late. We'd better go back to the *donga*.'

Neither of them uttered a word as they walked back
towards the *donga*. Cassandra was wishing that she had
died when the horse threw her or, better still, that the
Zulus had killed her this morning before Saul appeared
on the scene. She would not then have made the fatal
mistake of imagining that he was sacrificing himself for
love of her. She would not have gone after him, and
surrendered herself to him, and enabled him to trample
her gift of love so obscenely into the ground.

It was dark when they reached the *donga*. Gwylfa
Jones gave them a flat incurious look, but Bridget, who
was sitting close to the fire, huddled in one of the pelts,
began to weep with weak relief.

'Ah, Miss Cassandra, I've been that anxious . . . Mr
Jones would not leave me to go looking for you. Thanks
be to the Holy Virgin that no harm has befallen you!'

Hasn't it? Cassandra thought drearily, and tried to
smile. 'How much better you're looking, Bridget.'

'Mr Jones took such care of me,' the maid confided,
and blushed. 'He fed me broth like a baby, and washed
me hair and all. . . .'

Saul began to give them a brief account of what had
happened. When he had finished, Gwylfa Jones asked
curiously—'Will you tell me why the Zulus wanted to
harm their King's Blue-Eyed Induna?'

Saul nodded, and explained that he was out of favour
with Cetewayo. He ended with sardonic amusement,

'Yes, my self-centred friend, I know what you're thinking. My presence here endangers all of you. You're quite right, and I plan to leave you just as soon as I've eaten something.'

Jones was studying him with calculation. 'You are the only one who possesses a gun for which there is ammunition,' he observed.

Saul hesitated. 'If I can find my horse,' he said at last, 'I'll leave the gun and ammunition with you.'

'I don't follow you——'

'With a horse,' Saul explained, 'at least I'd be able to get away from any other chance-met Zulus. But on foot, my need for the gun would be greater than yours. So long as you aren't once again found in possession of the King's pelts, you have little to fear from the Zulus, and you could use my throwing spear for hunting. My wound would make me vulnerable for days; I couldn't possibly throw a spear. So unless my horse has returned to the *donga* I'll have to keep the gun.'

Jones pursed his lips. 'Well now, I did fancy I heard a horse whinnying once or twice today, somewhere in the *donga*. Did I not say so to you, Bridget?'

The maid looked uncertainly at him. 'The way of it was, Mr Jones, that *I* said I thought I'd heard a horse, but you said my nerves were playing tricks on me——'

'Naturally I said that. I didn't want you to worry, did I? For if the horse was back in the *donga*, then where was Miss Hudson? Do you see, Bridget?' He turned to Saul. 'Shall we go now and look for the animal?'

But two hours later they returned to the shallow cave in the *donga*, their search unsuccessful. 'You'd best wait until morning,' Jones told Saul. 'We'll soon find him then.'

Saul hesitated, frowning as he weighed matters up, his hand returning several times to his wounded shoulder. At last he nodded. 'Perhaps you're right.'

Cassandra cleared her throat. She addressed Saul without looking at him. 'Gwylfa Jones has been lying to you. I'm quite certain that the horse hasn't been heard in the *donga*, except in Bridget's imagination. He wants to keep you here for the night. He is hoping to steal your gun and ammunition while you sleep.'

'Miss Cassandra!' Bridget exclaimed, horrified. 'What a wicked slander! As for the horse, I *did* hear it, so I did!'

Saul smiled faintly. 'The morning light will tell whether or not you heard a real horse, Bridget. As for you, Cassandra—there's no need to feel concerned about any evil intentions Jones might have about my gun. I'm a light sleeper and my reflexes are swift. If anyone should be unwise enough to attempt removing the gun from me he might find the barrel discharged in his face.'

No more was said on the subject, but Gwylfa Jones gave Cassandra a dark look of dislike. She was quite sure that she had correctly gauged his intentions. Some uncharacteristic twinge of conscience had plagued him after he abandoned a desperately sick Bridget; now that he knew she had suffered no lasting ill he would want to go his own way again, ideally armed with Saul's gun. He might even give Bridget the choice whether or not to throw in her lot with him, but he would have no compunction about abandoning Cassandra for the second time, and he would certainly not wish to remain in Saul's dangerous presence for a moment longer than necessary.

Cassandra forced herself to remain awake that night, warned by some primitive instinct that went deeper even than her own feelings of pain and humiliation. She could not explain away her own fears, which seemed to have no logic. It was not even as if Saul were sleeping so soundly that he would fail to awaken if Jones made an attempt to seize the gun. On the contrary, he was twisting and turning, uttering muttered groans as his wound obviously pained him. Once, he shouted something in his sleep in the Zulu language; it had the corrosive sound of an oath. Then he began to groan again.

When the moth-grey light of dawn was washing into the shallow cave, Saul's groans became interspersed with mutterings, and Cassandra knew at last what she had instinctively been fearing. In the sub-tropical Zululand heat some rapid infection had grown and multiplied in his wound, and he was becoming delirious, as helpless as a baby. A furtive movement of the pelts which covered Gwylfa Jones alerted her, and before he could rise to his feet she had gained Saul's side. Saul offered no resistance when she took possession of the gun.

Gwylfa Jones came to squat on the ground close by. 'Since he's clearly too ill to leave us, Miss,' he said, '*we'd* best leave *him* as soon as possible. He'll be as comfortable here in the cave as anywhere.'

'We're not leaving him,' she said.

Jones made a sound of irritation. 'You heard what he said, Miss, about being a danger to everyone. What is he to you that you're willing to sacrifice all of us for his sake?'

'He's nothing to me.' *Nothing at all*, her heart mourned. *Some married woman in D'Urban has the right to him, if anyone has.*

Aloud, she went on, 'It was I who shot him, and the wound has become infected. If we left him here he'd die. I won't have his death on my conscience. He must be taken to Rorke's Drift. The missionary there will have medical supplies.'

'And how will he be taken to Rorke's Drift, Miss?'

Jones enquired with heavy irony. 'What Cinderella-coach do you propose to conjure out of thin air?'

'You'll have to go back for the wagon and oxen,' she said calmly.

'And if I refuse?'

'If you refuse I'll put a bullet in your knee, Mr Jones, and I'll go and look for the wagon and oxen myself, and take *both* of you to Rorke's Drift for treatment.'

He laughed suddenly. 'There's fierce, isn't it! You would do it too, I believe, Miss. Very well. I'll go for the wagon and oxen. But you'd better just pray that no Zulus find us with those pelts.'

Towards noon, Cassandra was anxiously beginning to wonder whether she had been wise to trust Jones to return with the wagon, instead of carrying on to Rorke's Drift on his own. And then she saw the cloud of dust on the horizon, and realised that he would not wish to stray far from the protection of their only gun, especially while in possession of King Cetewayo's pelts.

She had made Saul as comfortable as possible, washing and re-dressing his wound which was surrounded by angry red streaks. At times he became lucid enough, and then he would either curse her roundly for not leaving with Jones and letting him take his chances alone, or he would try to leave the cave himself, so that she and Bridget had to use all their combined strength to prevent him from rising.

But Saul was unconscious when Gwylfa Jones carried him to the wagon and settled him upon the pelts, and Cassandra watched him with deeply troubled eyes.

Her great fear was that gangrene would set in before they reached the mission at Rorke's Drift, and she would not allow Jones to stop and make camp until the moon was riding high in the sky and the oxen were exhausted. Then she remained on the wagon by Saul's side, and listened abstractedly to the conversation between Gwylfa Jones and Bridget outside.

There was a great deal of common ground between the two of them, it seemed. They shared a similar rural background; Jones's family, it appeared, had rented a hill farm in Wales while Bridget's parents had worked a small-holding in Ireland during her formative years.

'Things got bad on the farm,' she heard Jones say. 'It was a cruel spring and all the lambs died, and we could not pay the rent. So my Da' and my brothers went into the pits to earn some money. There was an explosion, do you see, and all three of them were killed. When Mam heard the news she had a stroke and died too. There was no compensation for me, being thirteen years old and deemed fit to earn my own living, and the farm was repossessed by the landlord. I wasn't about to sacrifice myself to the pits too, so I signed on for the Queen's shilling and awaited the opportunity to better myself. But there was precious little opportunity in Burma or India, where I served before coming here.'

Cassandra, listening to him, reflected that if Gwylfa Jones was an opportunist then, perhaps, there was some excuse for him.

Towards evening the next day a range of craggy, tumbled hills rose on the horizon, resembling, to the west, the shape of some crouching animal. They made camp in a dry ravine, but before the wagon descended into the ravine Saul had one of his lucid moments. He raised himself on his good elbow, and glanced out of the wagon flap as the vehicle zigzagged down the slope.

'Isandhlwana,'' he muttered.

'What's that?' Cassandra asked.

'Those hills—Isandhlwana. That's where we are.'

They spent an uneventful night in the ravine. Cassandra calculated that they were now some four miles from Rorke's Drift, and she examined Saul's wound anxiously as she dressed it, telling herself that it looked cleaner than it had before.

They were awakened in the morning by a totally unexpected sound—that of bugles, and it was coming from the Isandhlwana Hills. Jones muttered an oath under his breath. 'Her Majesty's Army . . . We had best get the wagon and oxen under cover of that overhanging rock, and pray that they do not pass this way on their march.'

But long after the wagon and oxen had been moved, there was still no sign of the Army, and the bugles had not sounded again.

Jones announced his intention of reconnoitring and Cassandra, who was consumed by nervous energy caused by their enforced inactivity, insisted on accompanying him.

'I could help you bring back some water,' she said. 'Bridget, keep an eye on Mr Parnell, and remember—the British Army are as much his enemies as the Zulus. Not that I think either are likely to come this way, however,' she added. 'The bugles must have been sounding from farther away than we thought.'

The plains seemed utterly deserted as she and Gwylfa Jones set off, scanning the horizons before making for the ubiquitous line of trees beyond which they knew they would find water.

They were filling their bags in the stream when the sound of furious hoofbeats caused them to turn in alarm. Four black soldiers led by a white officer and accompanied by several spare horses were approaching. Jones muttered to Cassandra, 'That's done it, Miss! You'd best leave the talking to me.'

The officer reined in his horse. 'You there—soldier! You're with the Twenty-fourth, aren't you? You're out of bounds! And what is that drummer boy doing out of uniform?'

Jones gave Cassandra a sidelong, desperate look.

'Well, sir, we—the way of it was, do you see——

'All right, never mind!' the officer interrupted impatiently. 'There's no time for explanations now. Your commanding officer will deal with you later. The two of you, share one of the spare horses.'

He glanced over his shoulder. 'Follow us back to camp as fast as you can. All hell is about to break loose—the Zulus are coming!'

CHAPTER
EIGHT

ONE of the black soldiers threw the reins of a spare horse at them. Jones caught them and turned to Cassandra. The officer said impatiently,

'Look sharp there, soldier! Give the boy a leg up and follow at the double!' He gave his own horse's rump a slap, and began to tittup away.

Cassandra scrambled into the saddle with Jones's help. 'We must get back to Saul and Bridget,' she said urgently, 'and make sure the wagon and oxen are hidden from sight of the Zulus. Quickly, while the soldiers are not paying attention to us!'

'Is it crazy you are, Miss?' Jones demanded tersely. 'A bullet through the head is what we'd both be getting, and no mistake, if we made one false move. *That* one may be a fool—in my experience, many of Her Majesty's officers are—but not so big a fool that he can't count. If we don't join him within two minutes he'll wheel around, and what do you think he would do if he saw us making off in the opposite direction? He would shoot us out of hand for deserting and showing cowardice in the face of the enemy!'

'That's outrageous!' Cassandra said. 'In the first place, he has no authority——'

'Oh yes, he has.' Jones's voice was cynical. 'He has all the authority of his class and his rank. He is an officer, look you, and the likes of you and me are expendable fodder. So just be quiet, Miss, while I do some thinking.'

'I will not be quiet! And neither will I be taken,

willy-nilly, to the British camp——'

Jones swore under his breath. 'Do you imagine *I* wish to return to my regiment, to be clapped in irons for deserting, with only the hangman's noose to look forward to?'

'Well, *do* something!'

'I intend to, Miss. See that gully yonder, with its growth of scrub and thorn trees? I'll make a break for it within its cover, and hope we may be a safe distance away before the officer and his native soldiers realise that we are missing.'

But when they reached the gully Cassandra and Jones were so effectively hemmed in between the other riders that it would have been impossible to make a break without immediately drawing attention to themselves.

'What now?' Cassandra asked desperately, when the gully was behind them and the other riders had fanned out beyond earshot.

'Now we resign ourselves to the inevitable, Miss,' he said grimly, 'and hope that something will come up.'

'*You* may resign yourself, but I shan't! *I* am not a soldier, bound by military regulations. As soon as we come within earshot again, I shall tell the officer that I am not a drummer boy, but a young lady——'

Jones made a derisive sound in his throat. 'And how will you account for being in the company of a Queen's infantryman, and yourself got up like a boy, Miss?'

'I don't know . . . I'll think of something. I could tell a half-truth. I could say that I had escaped from the Zulus, and was trying to join my cousin at his mission, when I met up with you——'

'And that will make it perfectly plain, won't it, Miss, that I had deserted from my regiment.' Jones's voice was hard. 'That officer thinks we were merely out of bounds, sky-larking by the river when we should have been with our company. My only hope is that with the

Zulus coming and the camp at sixes and sevens, no one will pay much attention to us. But if you tell your story, Miss, the officer will be in no doubt that I had deserted. I will be placed under guard as soon as we reach the camp.'

'Well, you knew the risks you were taking when you deserted,' Cassandra pointed out. 'Good lord, I couldn't carry off the pretence of being a drummer boy! Even you must see that——'

'No drumming will be required while the fighting lasts, Miss,' he said with heavy humour.

She ignored the remark. 'I must get back to the ravine! Bridget won't know what to do, and Saul—Saul might die of his fever——'

'Now you see here, Miss,' Gwylfa Jones interrupted. 'You don't care what happens to me, but you *do* care what happens to the Zulu King's Blue-Eyed Induna. You cut up rough and draw attention to my deserting, and I'll tell them exactly where they can lay hands on the man they wish to try as a spy and a traitor!'

Cassandra turned her head swiftly to look at him, and his expression told her that it was no idle threat. 'What you're suggesting is madness,' she said in desperation. 'Once the skirmish with the Zulus is over it won't be long before it's discovered that I'm a girl, and then it is bound to come out that you are a deserter. In the meantime Saul could die for lack of medical attention——'

'There's a pity, isn't it.' His voice roughened. 'I matter to no one, Miss, except to myself. That has been the way of it since my Mam died. And that being so, I have to look out for myself. So don't ask me to make sacrifices for the Blue-Eyed Induna.'

Cassandra was silent, her thoughts furiously racing. As they followed the officer and his retinue of black soldiers the ground was rising steeply towards a lofty range. They skirted another gully, barren and rock-strewn this time, affording no cover. Facing them now was a craggy spur of rock jutting out from the larger formation, and at the foot of this, on the southern slope of the Isandhlwana Hills, the British were encamped.

News of the Zulus' approach had obviously already reached the camp, for even from this distance they could see that it was a seething mass of activity, with field guns being deployed, commissariat wagons trundling out with supplies, and a rocket battery being set up in position. Horses and red-jacketed soldiery added to the frantic mosaic.

Jones spoke again, his tone more conciliatory now. 'Leave whatever talking is to be done to me, Miss, and stay close. Once the Zulus attack and no one has time to pay attention to us, we'll try to get away in the confusion. That is our only chance.'

Cassandra didn't reply. She scarcely gave a thought to the possible danger of finding herself involved in a skirmish with the Zulus; all she could think of was Saul, whose danger was threefold—from Zulu and British alike, and from the fever which was consuming him.

As they rode into camp, the officer and his native scouts were besieged for news of the enemy's movements, and no one had attention to spare for Cassandra and Jones. They dismounted and began to mingle with the crowd.

The four infantry companies of the Twenty-fourth Foot Regiment were taking up position ahead of the camp, beyond the artillery and the mounted contingent. The surging tide of soldiers and native reservists were entirely preoccupied with the coming engagement; the atmosphere in the camp was one of nervous excitement and anticipation of what would be the first encounter between Britons and Zulus. It seemed scarcely likely that anyone would have time or attention to spare for Gwylfa Jones, even if he was suddenly recognised as a deserter.

From the remarks passing to and fro around them, Cassandra and Jones gathered the information that Lord Chelmsford had previously left with the main column to look for the enemy, but that the force of six hundred Imperial infantry, three hundred and fifty cavalry, nine hundred foot levies—not to mention two field guns and the rocket battery—which had been left to guard the camp under the command of Colonel Durnford, were considered to be more than sufficient with which to resist attack

Durnford's mounted men were being divided into three bodies and were preparing to ride out to engage the enemy. The main fear of the foot-soldiers seemed to be that the Zulus would be beaten before they, too, had had their share of the fighting.

'Do you see that stretch of rough ground behind the hospital tents, Miss?' Jones murmured, inclining his head.

Beyond where the mounted infantry were taking up their positions Cassandra could see, through the gaps between the hospital tents, an area of long waving grass and scattered boulders.

'We'll hide out there, Miss. I'll go first, and you follow shortly. If anyone challenges you, tell them you're looking for Don, Lieutenant Daly's dog.'

She nodded, and loitered for a while before following Jones through the milling soldiers towards the area of rough ground. As she came abreast of the hospital tents a thought struck her.

There would be ample medical supplies inside those tents. Drugs with which to fight Saul's fever ...

An orderly appeared in the doorway of the nearest tent, and Cassandra hastily turned away, and pretended to be heading off a skittish horse which had escaped from the animal enclosure.

No one challenged her, or noticed as she melted into the rough terrain behind the hospital tents. Jones was lying on his stomach in the long grass, and she flung herself down beside him.

She watched the dedication, indeed the enthusiasm, with which the ordinary soldiers were going about their duties, preparing to fight for their Queen and country.

'Why did you desert?' she addressed Jones abruptly. 'Was it because you feared being killed in battle? And yet—you must have known the dangers when you decided to become a soldier. I cannot believe that you enlisted solely as a means of seeking your fortune——'

'I enlisted as a boy soldier because the Queen's shilling and a daily ration seemed better than starving in the Welsh valleys, Miss. And I was an innocent then. I dreamt of glory.'

He made a derisive sound. 'I did not know, do you see, that there could be no question of glory for the likes of me. The glory was reserved for the officers, just as the well-filled brandy decanters and the rations served up in silver dishes were reserved for their mess tents, while such as I squatted on a knapsack under the stars and ate hard-tack and bully beef with their fingers.'

'But surely the glory lies in serving one's country——'

Jones laughed shortly. 'It is very hard to think of serving one's country, Miss, when you are marching on half-rations in the fierce heat of the day or in torrential rain, through mud and dust and swollen rivers, up hill and down dale, and at the end of the day you have to help erect the officers' tents before you can dig a shelter-trench to serve as your own bed for the night.'

'In other words,' Cassandra commented, 'you deserted because you were resentful of the officers' privileges——?'

'No, Miss, that is not why I deserted. It came to me gradually that those officers, those men with the power of life or death over me, who could order me to fight and kill some poor devil I had no quarrel with; who could order me to be flogged or hanged if I did not obey them blindly—it came to me that most of them were far more stupid or ignoble or superficial than I. And I began to question to myself what they were requiring me to do, and why.'

He jerked his head towards the camp. 'Those poor swaddies there, preparing to engage the Zulus—what do you suppose they will be doing it all for? Have you asked yourself, Miss—*Why declare war on the Zulus at all*? They cannot be a threat to our country or our interests, and Queen Victoria could scarcely covet their own inhospitable country as part of her Empire. So what is it all for?

'I'll tell you, Miss. Those soldiers are preparing to lay down their otherwise valueless lives, if need be, because Lord Chelmsford had ambitions to collect more military honours. But for the rank and file there is only the prospect of an assegai through the belly. There will be no honours for them, no glory. They will be remembered by no one, and no one will question the reason for their deaths. And that, Miss, is why I deserted.'

Cassandra had been listening to his passionate speech with mixed feelings. She studied him. 'Where did you receive your education, Mr Jones?'

He shrugged. 'I learnt my letters from my Mam, and taught myself to read and write.'

She had always realised that he was of high intelligence, and she could not help thinking that it was as well, perhaps, that the majority of Her Majesty's enlisted men did not share his reasoning.

She stiffened as firing began to sound all along the

crest of the hill. The mounted men who had gone out to engage the enemy had commenced the attack.

The frantic activity in the camp had ceased, and every man was at his post, awaiting orders. Where before everything had been chaos, order now reigned, and Cassandra thought fearfully that if the mounted troops demolished the Zulus during this skirmish she and Jones would not be able to get away unnoticed.

Suddenly the sound of firing intensified. The men guarding the rocky spur were in action. Then above the sound of firing came volleys of shouted commands, interspersed with oaths. Cassandra raised herself cautiously and peered through the long grass.

The mounted men were retreating back to camp, and the Zulus were swarming after them like bees. It was only too obvious that the size of the enemy force had been woefully underestimated. In defiance of heavy artillery fire the Zulus were pushing forward rapidly.

But in spite of their superior force the enemy fell in hundreds, mown down by the far more sophisticated weapons of the British. Incredibly, the Zulus still came on in apparently undiminished numbers. Nothing seemed to deter them. As rank upon rank of the foremost fell, others pressed steadily forward to take their place, with what seemed like suicidal zeal.

Cassandra and Jones no longer tried to remain hidden, for the camp was far too preoccupied with the danger facing it to pay attention to them. But this was no time to attempt a getaway. A black, heaving mass of Zulus cut off any hope of escape.

They were coming far more quickly than the quartermasters could dispense ammunition. Runners from the line arrived hot and breathless for stores, but there was confusion at the reserve wagons, and the quartermasters were retarded by the heavily nailed and banded ammunition boxes. The troops were obliged to reduce

fire while the ammunition crates were broken open in a
frenzy of frustrated fury, by means of rifle butts and
bayonets and anything else which came to hand.

This pause in the firing was what the Zulus had been
waiting for. One after another the regiments rose, roaring their disdain, stamping their feet and beating their
assegais against their shields.

The cry of *'uSuthu!'*—Cetewayo's war-cry, which
Cassandra had heard before at Ulundi—rent the air as
they surged forward. The atmosphere was thick with
smoke from the Martini-Henry's as the British replied.

Still the Zulus came on, like a moving, unbreachable
black wall, ploughing their way through the corpses of
their own dead, stamping their feet on the ground,
rattling their assegais against their shields.

'uSuthu!' they roared, and added a contemptuous
challenge to their white enemy, *'Yize, yize, yize!'*

Somewhere, a bugle sounded 'Retire'. In the camp,
the fighting was now hand-to-hand. The redcoats
scarcely had time to fix bayonets. Zulus hurled corpses
on the blades of those same bayonets before rushing in
for the kill. Among the overwhelming blacks, the redcoats stood out patchily, like exotic splashes of colour
on a dark ground. The camp was strewn with corpses
from both sides.

'Poor devils,' Gwylfa Jones muttered tautly
beside Cassandra. 'Poor stupid bloody devils. All of
them . . .'

In the ravine, the battle sounds from the Isandhlwana
Hills had slowly been penetrating the mists of Saul
Parnell's brain, until nagging instinct told him that
he could no longer submit to the fever, that he was
needed.

He struggled to a sitting position, and focused with
difficulty on Bridget's scared, pale face.

'Jones—Cassandra—where are they?' he demanded.

'Sure and I don't know, sir, and it's that feared I'm becomin'.' She twisted her hands together. 'They went out early this morning, to see what was afoot, and not a sign of them has there been since.'

Her face began to swim before his gaze, and he made a superhuman effort to fight against the effects of the fever. 'They went—towards the hills?' he muttered.

'They did that, sir.'

Saul closed his eyes in concentration. 'The King's amulet, Bridget—was your mistress wearing it? If she was, then it would keep her safe from the Zulus, at least . . .'

'Yon pagan necklace, sir?' he heard Bridget respond. ''Tis somewhere on the wagon.'

He swore weakly under his breath. 'Fetch it, please.'

While she was gone he forced himself to rise, and began to move about slowly in grim concentration, compelling circulation back into his legs, keeping the effects of his fever at bay by sheer force of will.

Bridget returned with King Cetewayo's beaded badge of safe-conduct. He took it from her, and thrust it over his head so that it lay, gaudy and incongruous, against his shirt. Next he asked for food and water, and doggedly compelled himself to eat every scrap of the dry rusks she handed him. He would need every ounce of energy it was possible for him to command.

'Beggin' your pardon, sir,' Bridget said, 'but what is it you're after doin'?'

'I'm going to look for them, Bridget.'

'But sir—how will you find them?'

'God alone knows. They may be dead, caught in the crossfire. Or the Zulus may have captured them.' He paused to rally his failing strength. 'If the Zulus have not killed them outright, then there's a chance—just a chance . . . In any event, I mean to try.'

Bridget's expression became set and defiant, 'I'm coming too, sir.'

'No, you are not——'

'Miss Cassandra ordered me to stay with you, sir.'

He shook his head, as much to clear it as to emphasise his point. 'You can't come, Bridget. It would be too dangerous.' Seeing her determined expression, he added, 'The King's amulet will only protect the wearer.'

'I don't care, sir.'

'Bridget, for the love of heaven! This whole plan is crazy—not that there *is* a plan. I don't know what I mean to do, only that I must do something. I am probably just as crazy——'

'Indeed, sir, beggin' your pardon. But I still mean to go with you, for all that.'

He uttered a short laugh. 'Very well. But let us at least *try* and plan something.'

After some thought, he decided that no purpose could be served by attempting stealth. He and Bridget hitched the oxen to the wagon, having at first removed all of the King's incriminating pelts from it. Then they began to travel towards the Isandhlwana Hills. At times Bridget had to take over the driving as he fought waves of near-delirium which threatened to overcome him.

It was some time after noon that they came within sight of the fighting, and Saul could see at once that the British were about to be decimated. The Zulus were sweeping through their lines and the British, hopelessly outnumbered, were retreating before the black horde.

The Zulus had become aware of the approaching wagon at their rear, and several warriors came running towards it, their spears aloft. But as soon as they saw the King's amulet about Saul's neck they lowered their weapons.

Saul thought as rapidly as his high temperature would allow. He had recognised this particular regiment of the King's army; it was the inGobamakhosi, a young regiment with its own distinctive shields. As far as he knew he was not known by sight to any of its impis or generals. He hoped that his haggard pallor and several days' growth of beard would also help to serve as some disguise.

Speaking in halting Zulu, and fingering the King's amulet, he explained that he was a missionary, and that with the King's blessing and consent he was taking his two young sons out of Zululand and danger But one of his sons had gone to fetch water that morning, and had not returned.

The Zulus disclaimed any knowledge of a white youth, and agreed that Saul could follow their lines into the British camp, in the hope of gaining some news of his missing 'son'.

When all this had been translated to Bridget, she asked with a frown, 'And what about Gwylfa Jones, sir? How will you explain him away to the Zulus supposin we find them alive?'

Saul shrugged. 'He is a soldier There is nothing could do to save him '

From their hiding place behind the hospital tents Cassandra and Gwylfa Jones watched the slaughter Some of the redcoats were desperately trying to escape on horseback, only to have their mounts brought down by a flying spear. Others were engaged in hand-to-hand combat with the Zulus.

Cassandra witnessed, appalled, the hospital tents being ripped apart, so that even the sick and wounded were forced to fight the unequal battle for their lives Equipment was broken up and medicines scattered to the winds. She thought of the hopeless, crazy plans she had been toying with, plans to steal medicine for Saul, and her mouth twisted. She would never see Saul again for there was no possible way in which she and Jones could escape. Strangely, she felt no fear, even though Zulu warriors were systematically ramming their spears into each prone white body on the ground to make sure that it really was dead

And then, just as she had known it would, came the moment when two Zulus crashed their way through the long grass towards them They must have caught a glimpse of Gwylfa Jones's red coat

But she had no intention of being impaled where she lay. She rose to her feet, and awaited the Zulus with dignity. Jones, uttering a resigned curse, rose too

The Zulus were within inches of them when she heard Saul's voice shouting something she could not understand. She thought it was a delusion, something conjured up by her mind in this, the last moment of her life. Then a sound of astonishment from Gwylfa Jones told her that he, too, had heard and recognised Saul's voice.

The Zulus stayed their hands, and turned. Saul was wending his way erratically through the swirling black mass which was now looting the camp and breaking open ammunition boxes. Cassandra understood nothing, least of all why the Zulus were allowing the hunted Blue-Eyed Induna such free passage. She only knew that she was to be united with Saul before she died.

Running to meet him, she flung herself in his arms. 'Oh Saul,' she said incoherently, 'I know you don't love me—but I'm glad that we're to die together——'

He brushed her cheek briefly with his lips. 'We assuredly will die,' he muttered. 'if you do not restrain yourself. You are supposed to be my son.'

He turned his head, making a beckoning gesture, and for the first time Cassandra saw Bridget. As her maid joined them, Saul drew her to him also, so that he stood

with an arm about each of his 'sons'. He began to
address the surrounding Zulus, fingering the King's
amulet all the while.

They nodded agreement. Two of them moved
towards Gwylfa Jones, their spears aloft, and Bridget
gave a little cry. Saul, looking grey-faced, addressed
the Welshman.

'I am sorry. There is nothing I can do—no lie I can
tell—which will save you . . .'

His voice faded, and he began to sag between
Cassandra and Bridget as the superhuman reserves
of strength on which he had been drawing finally
deserted him. The two girls could do no more than
break his fall.

Saul's collapse had diverted the Zulus' attention from
Gwylfa Jones. They looked down at the unconscious
man wearing their King's amulet, and their dilemma
was obvious. They were under an obligation to see that
he received help and support, and yet they could not
encumber themselves with a sick 'missionary' and his
two sons.

Gwylfa Jones's agile mind had summed up the situation very quickly and accurately. By means of mime, he
indicated to the Zulus that if he was spared, he would
make himself responsible for the sick man and the
'youths'.

The Zulus conferred among themselves, and then
agreed. Saul was carried to the wagon, and supplies
looted from the camp were piled into it. Jones climbed
into the driver's seat; Bridget took the lead rope while
Cassandra cradled Saul's head on her lap, making him
as comfortable as possible.

The black mass of Zulus, swarming like ants from a
disturbed ant-heap, parted and allowed the wagon safe
passage. News of the King's amulet had been passed on
from impi to impi.

Saul's burst of activity had taken its toll of his system, for towards evening his fever was very high, and Cassandra was filled with fearful concern. But they were forced to make camp, for the oxen needed rest.

Among the looted supplies given to them by the Zulus were tinned meat, and a flask of brandy which Cassandra seized upon with gratitude. As soon as Saul was lucid enough to co-operate, she held the flask to his lips. The spirit revived him sufficiently to enable him to eat some of the tinned meat, and afterwards he appeared to her to be sinking into a normal sleep.

After she had left him, she joined Bridget and Jones by the camp fire. 'It has just come to me,' Gwylfa Jones said reflectively. 'Those poor devils—every man jack of them killed by the Zulus—they were almost all serving with the Twenty-fourth. *My* regiment.'

No one said anything. Cassandra remembered what Saul had once said about the British wanting hostilities with the Zulus, so that they could try out their sophisticated new weapons. If that really was true, then they had paid a terrible price for any experience they gained. . . .

She shuddered. She would never forget what she had seen and experienced. Her lips moved in a silent prayer that at Rorke's Drift, safely with the Reverend Otto Wit, the war would not touch them again. Saul could recover in the mission hospital, and the Swedish missionary would not be concerned with the fact that he was wanted by both the British and the Zulus. Even Gwylfa Jones would be safe, for the Reverend Wit would not care that he was a deserter.

Late the next day they crossed the Buffalo River at Rorke's Drift, which was a shallow ford. A road flanked by scrub led them to a rocky shelf, beyond which they could see the roofs of the mission and the Reverend Wit's residence through a screen of tall, straggly trees.

At almost the same instant as they saw the Army tents between the two stone buildings, and the supply wagons drawn up beyond them, they became aware of the armed redcoat guards who were galloping towards them.

Gwylfa Jones began to swear, monotonously and with dull disbelief, in Welsh.

The mission had been requisitioned. They had escaped from one British camp straight into another·

CHAPTER
NINE

CASSANDRA'S mouth was dry with fear. If the Rorke's Drift mission had been occupied by Cetewayo's army, things would have looked marginally less black for them, for the sight of the King's amulet would at least have influenced those Zulus who did not know Cetewayo's white Induna by sight.

From the British Army, neither Saul nor Gwylfa Jones could expect any mercy. And the red-coated guards were almost level with the leading oxen in the span by now.

Saul raised himself on one elbow. Last night seemed to have been the crisis point of his fever, or perhaps the brandy and tinned meat had enabled his system to begin the process of recovery, for his condition showed a marked change this morning. But even if he had not still been physically weak, there was nothing he could have done against the armed guards approaching them so inexorably.

'Play for time,' he muttered. 'Try bluff. Embroider my story. I'm a missionary—Jones a survivor of Isandhlawana.' He grinned faintly. 'I'd better be unconscious, I think. Less recognisable that way ...'

Cassandra relayed his message to Jones, who nodded grimly. Then the guards drew level with them.

Jones leant down from the driver's seat. 'There is a sick man on the wagon,' he told the guards. 'The Reverend—Seth Parsons. Do you have medical supplies?'

One of the guards said, 'We have better than that.

Wit's house has been commandeered as a hospital. But what is your name, soldier, and what are you doing with these people, instead of being with your company?'

'I shall give my explanations to your commanding officer,' Jones said grandly.

The guards circled the wagon, lifted the flap and assured themselves that it did hold a man who was apparently unconscious. When Jones told them that the two 'youths' were the missionary's sons, they appeared to accept his story and they gave the order for the wagon to continue on its way while they rode alongside.

'Our luck has held this far,' Jones commented grimly. 'I'm hoping they won't want to be burdened with a sick missionary. Perhaps I can persuade them to give us some medical supplies and food, and allow me to escort the three of you to D'Urban.'

Cassandra said nothing. *Luck*, she thought. How long could it be expected to hold?

At the foot of the Oskarberg, a bleak and rocky outcrop, stood the two stone buildings belonging to the Swedish mission. The larger, which resembled an enormous barn and had probably been the mission building, was now apparently used to hold Army stores Set slightly forward from this was the dwelling house, now doing duty as a hospital. In an area close by, the British were encamped

One of the guards had ridden on ahead to alert an officer, so that by the time the wagon arrived in the camp Lieutenant Gonville Bromhead was waiting for them. Gwylfa Jones, Bridget and Cassandra climbed from the wagon.

Lieutenant Bromhead was a man in his mid-thirties, with handsome features and a bushy moustache. Apparently hard of hearing, he made Jones repeat his carefully rehearsed story several times The officer's frown deepened as he took in the account of the battle of

Isandhlwana

'Are you trying to convince me,' he exploded, 'that a band of savages wiped out almost your entire regiment? I don't believe it!'

'It's quite true,' Cassandra intervened, adding 'sir', when she remembered that she was supposed to be a youth.

The officer turned his scowling gaze on her. 'And what do you know about it, eh? From the soldier's account you and your father and your brother were miles away from Isandhlwana when he came upon you! This whole story stinks to high heaven!'

He turned back to Jones, staring at him. 'Jones . . . Jones. *Gwylfa* Jones. Odd name. Not the Jones part, of course. The British Army is crawling with 'em. But I've heard your name before, somewhere. Gwylfa Jones, of the Twenty-fourth Infantry. Your name cropped up at a mess dinner one night. Can't remember why, but it was something to your discredit——'

Cassandra felt sick with dismay. Now that Lieutenant Bromhead's suspicions had been aroused, it could not be long before the whole story came out.

And then, almost as if a malicious Fate wished to underline the collapse of all their hopes, a familiar figure threaded his way towards them. It was Martin, looking officious and self-important. The one person she had not bargained on seeing at Rorke's Drift was her cousin. Martin, who would recognise Saul on sight . . .

'I've heard that one of my brother missionaries has been brought to the camp, Lieutenant,' Martin began, and broke off, staring at Cassandra. 'I know you from somewhere, don't I?'

She shook her head and stared expressionlessly back at him, in the slim hope that he would fail to connect his girl cousin with the dusty and dishevelled youth in front of him. After all, he hadn't seen her for five years . . .

But he suddenly exclaimed, '*Cassandra*! Good Lord above!' Incredulity, horror and distaste crossed his face in rapid succession.

Through waves of dismay, Cassandra heard Lieutenant Bromhead say—'By Jove, a girl, eh? I knew the story stank of fish! Who is she, Coleman?'

'My cousin,' Martin said stiffly. 'Apparently masquerading as a boy. I need hardly tell you how mortified I am to find her in these circumstances, Lieutenant. If she has indeed been travelling in the company of a missionary, I cannot think what he was about, allowing her to—degrade herself in this manner!'

'You're quite right, Coleman.' Lieutenant Bromhead nodded grimly. 'And I don't think a bona fide missionary is involved in this at all. Now that I come to consider it, there *are* no other missionaries near this part of the border, apart from yourself and the Reverend Ottto Wit.'

'What are you doing at Rorke's Drift, Martin?' Cassandra asked, desperately playing for time, vainly trying to distract attention from Saul. It was a pathetic ploy, and she knew it.

Her cousin said austerely, 'I wonder that you have the temerity to question *my* movements, Cassandra. However . . . I sought refuge with the Reverend Otto Wit across the Zululand border when hostilities seemed imminent.'

'You must have guessed that I would have set out for Magwana,' Cassandra said. 'Did it never occur to you to go back to Zululand and look for me?'

'No, it did not. I do not give way to impulse, Cassandra. I had sent word for you to await me in D'Urban; even if I had known that you had been foolish enough to travel to Zululand, it would not have helped you if I *had* set off hot-foot after you. However,' he added, 'I prayed for you daily.'

Cassandra uttered a sound which was halfway between a laugh and a sob. *'He would leave you in the hands of the Lord,'* Saul had said scathingly of Martin. *'And then if anything happened to you, that would be God's will.'*

Her cousin went on censoriously, 'I must say, Cassandra, that you might have considered my position and my reputation before you lent yourself to this indecent masquerade!'

'Don't you think,' she countered, 'that I might have been forced into it by dire necessity?'

Lieutenant Bromhead had been listening to them with barely concealed impatience. He was about to interrupt their exchange when a commotion from the animal stockade forced their attention. A rider was galloping hard through the camp on the back of an unsaddled horse, his hands fastened in its mane.

'What the devil——' Lieutenant Bromhead began.

Joyous disbelief coursed through Cassandra. Saul had taken swift advantage of the respite she had contrived for him; he had obviously slipped unnoticed from the back of the wagon and stolen quietly away to the animal enclosure for a horse. Now, as she watched, he evaded a couple of guards who came running, and jumped a stone wall beyond the two buildings. He had disappeared among the scrub before Lieutenant Bromhead could order the guards to fire at him.

It was a good half-hour later before it was finally established that the rider had been Cetewayo's white chief. Jones stuck doggedly to his story that as far as he was concerned, he had fallen into company with a sick missionary and his two sons; Bridget and Cassandra refused to say anything until they felt sure that Saul would have covered a safe distance on his stolen horse.

Gwylfa Jones was taken away for more intensive

questioning by Lieutenant Bromhead while Cassandra
and Bridget were put in charge of the two missionaries
in the camp, Martin and the Reverend Otto Wit.

Cassandra's feelings were mixed. She gave fervent
thanks for Saul's timely escape, and yet she could not
help mourning the fact that he had gone out of her life
for good. In the meantime she had to endure Martin's
censorious lectures on her own behaviour.

He was still handsome, she thought dispassionately,
if one appraised his features separately. But what came
across most strongly, totally cancelling out his good
looks, was a quality of smugness, of pious self-
satisfaction and humbug. She knew instinctively that
he was more concerned with what the world would say
of her than he was about any of the dangers she might
have experienced during the past weeks.

After they had eaten, Cassandra and Bridget were
again summoned to Lieutenant Bromhead's tent, to be
questioned this time about their knowledge of Gwylfa
Jones. Doggedly, they maintained the story that they
had only met him after his escape from Isandhlwana.

'You and your friends,' Lieutenant Bromhead told
Cassandra grimly, 'have offered me so many lies since I
first made your acquaintance that I cannot accept anything you tell me. The four of you are clearly in a
conspiracy of some sort——'

He stopped. From outside came the sound of furious
hoofbeats, and then the noise of a scuffle, together with
shouting voices. The flap of the tent moved aside as
Saul, closely followed by two guards, almost fell into
the tent.

Cassandra whispered his name, staring at him in
utter dismay. His face was haggard, his hair clinging
damply to his forehead, and he seemed to sway slightly
as the two guards seized each of his arms. He should
have been miles away. What could have gone wrong?

'Saul Parnell, sir,' one of the guards explained. 'It appears he changed his mind and came back.'

Lieutenant Bromhead opened his mouth to speak, but Saul forestalled him.

'Be quiet,' he commanded unevenly, 'and *listen*. The Zulus—are coming. They're advancing on Rorke's Drift in a mass. I can get the civilians—the girls and the missionaries—out of here to safety——'

Lieutenant Bromhead looked at the guards. 'Have any of the scouts reported aught afoot?'

'No, sir. It could be a trick ...'

'Yes,' the officer agreed grimly.

'You fool!' Saul flung at him. 'You'll have enough on your hands—when the Zulus arrive—without the responsibility of civilians——'

'Take him away,' Bromhead said to the guards. 'Have him confined in one of the rooms in the hospital under armed guard——'

'*Damn you!*' Saul shouted desperately. 'I'll take them to Helpmekaar if you wish—to the British fort! I'll surrender myself to the commanding officer there——'

Lieutenant Bromhead merely shook his head impassively.

Cassandra felt sick with anxiety and dread. Saul had made his tremendous sacrifice for nothing. It was entirely like him that he had made it without any thought for himself.

She turned on the officer. 'Can't you see that he's telling the truth? Why would he have come back here of his own free will if he hadn't seen the Zulus advancing on Rorke's Drift?'

Before Bromhead could answer another officer entered the tent, his manner one of urgency.

'See who we have here, Chard!' Lieutenant Bromhead cried triumphantly. 'King Cetewayo's

Blue-Eyed Induna himself——'

'Never mind that,' Lieutenant Chard dismissed the subject with a tense, impatient gesture. 'I have grave news. I was inspecting the pontoons on the river when two riders came galloping up, subalterns with the Natal Native Contingent. They've ridden from Isandhlwana. By the grace of God they got through the Zulu guard. It's all true, Gonny—we've sustained a terrible defeat at Isandhlwana, and the Zulus are marching on Rorke's Drift.'

'*Now* will you let me take the girls and the missionaries out of here?' Saul demanded.

The two officers exchanged glances. 'No,' Bromhead said at last, regretfully. 'Neither Lieutenant Chard nor I have the authority to let you go. You are wanted on charges of treason and espionage, and we have to abide by the regulations. Guards, take him away and see that he is securely confined.'

In anguish, Cassandra watched the guards drag Saul away. Then she turned to the officers. 'If you are thinking of sending me away under the escort of anyone other than Saul Parnell, let me tell you that my maid and I will refuse to co-operate!'

Lieutenant Chard grinned wryly. 'My dear Miss Hudson, we couldn't spare any of our soldiers to escort you. Besides, it's probably too late already. The Zulus are said to be a mere half-hour's march away.'

Bromhead frowned at his brother officer. 'You think we should stay and face the enemy? The camp isn't prepared for a mass assault——'

'I don't see that we have any alternative. At least we can learn from the mistakes at Isandhlwana, and attempt to form a laager——' Lieutenant Chard broke off, and turned to Cassandra and Bridget. 'You two young ladies,' he said, 'will please excuse us. We have vital matters to discuss.'

Outside in the camp, there was an air of palpable excitement in the air. By now everyone had a version of what had happened, usually grossly distorted, and everyone speculated on what was to happen shortly.

The camp was wide open to attack, and poorly manned with only one company and a small party of native levies. There were also some thirty-odd sick men in the hospital, who could not easily be moved in case of a retreat.

The two officers emerged from the tent and gave the order for the men to fall in and stand to attention. Briefly, Lieutenant Chard announced that they were to stay and fight; there was no time to retreat before the Zulus. The first priority was to fortify the camp as strongly as possible.

Quickly, the tents were struck. Then every single pair of available hands, including those of Cassandra and Bridget, were pressed into constructing a defensive barrier.

The only building materials quickly and readily available were the stocks of biscuit-boxes and sacks of mealies stored in the requisitioned mission building. These were speedily dragged out, and used to fashion a defensive wall.

The sun was low in the sky, the barrier still incomplete, when a great shout went up The look-out on the Oskarberg had sighted the Zulu regiments through field glasses.

The tension was almost tangible. The soldiers hurriedly snatched up their rifles and bayonets. Martin, looking white-faced and tense, tried to order Cassandra and Bridget to repair to comparative safety behind the requisitioned store-house with him, where the Reverend Otto Wit had already taken shelter.

Cassandra ignored her cousin's commands, and set out to look for Lieutenant Bromhead instead. She found him staring fixedly at Gwylfa Jones.

'Got it!' the officer said abruptly. 'Remember where I'd heard your name! One of your company's officers. I suppose he's dead now, poor chap. However . . . I knew it was something discreditable. You're a——'

The word 'deserter' was drowned by a sudden chaotic scramble as first the mounted natives rode pell-mell from the vedette posts, closely followed by the Kaffirs stationed at the outpost.

The mass desertion caught everyone by surprise. Then one officer and several N.C.O's set off after them. But they were not trying to head off the deserting natives, as was first assumed; they were joining them. They scrambled over the barricades in the wake of the Kaffirs and mounted troops, and Cassandra saw that the Reverend Otto Wit had belatedly joined them. Martin hesitated for a moment, as if he, too, toyed with the idea of flight.

Bromhead turned away with a contemptuous shrug, and stared at Gwylfa Jones. His deepening frown made it clear what he was thinking. Jones had deserted once; he could very easily have deserted again today, especially as he had been unmasked. And yet he had made no attempt to do so. In Gonville Bromhead's mind it obviously did not add up.

Cassandra claimed the officer's attention. 'My maid and I wish to help in the hospital,' she said.

'Why, that's most——' he began, and broke off, staring suspiciously at her. 'If you have any notion of helping Saul Parnell to escape, young lady——'

He was interrupted by a shout. The vanguard of the Zulu regiments had appeared in sight around the Oskarberg. Within minutes a force of some six hundred Zulus advanced on the rear of the mission while the remainder swept around the west of the outpost. They were an awe-inspiring sight.

'Escape would be pointless,' Cassandra told Bromhead. 'The Zulus want him as much as the British do. Do we have your permission to help at the hospital?'

He nodded. 'Report to Surgeon Major Reynolds.'

The hospital, formerly the Wit residence, had been constructed in such a way that a verandah was the only means of communicating between some of the rooms. All of the rooms had been pressed into service as hospital wards. At every possible loophole throughout the building soldiers were stationed in defence of the hospital.

Cassandra and Bridget busied themselves with nursing duties, thus making the orderlies available to help in the fighting. But all the time she performed routine tasks Cassandra's mind was picking at the problem of finding out where Saul was being held in the hospital, and somehow helping him to get away.

Outside, the Zulu warriors had found the gaps in the barricade which there had been no time to fill. They fell upon them in a swirling black torrent. Elsewhere the Zulus ignored the bodies of their comrades falling all about them, and began to clamber on the barricades. A volley of shots sent them reeling back.

Standing shoulder to shoulder, the men under Lieutenant Bromhead held their line intact. Like automatons they fired and reloaded, fired and reloaded, and plunged their bayonets into those Zulus who ignored the bullets and kept coming at them with crazy valour.

The air was alive with the crash of gunfire, with shouted oaths, with high-pitched yells of triumph or of anguish and with the swish-swish of flying assegais.

The barricades were holding, but the camp's position was desperate. With suicidal bravery, the Zulus advanced in wave upon wave. As their compatriots fell around them they simply crawled through the carpet of corpses, yelling and impervious. In places the barricades were, ironically, strengthened by the sheer mass of Zulu corpses piled against it from the other side.

But at other places the Zulus broke through the now bloodstained mealie bags, and then the hospital was under siege. No help could be expected from the hard-pressed soldiers who were defending the perimeter.

'Evacuate the patients!' the order came from Surgeon Major Reynolds.

Cassandra abandoned all pretence at caution or subtlety. She hurried to look for Saul. The Zulus were trying to storm the verandah of the hospital, and were held off by a thin line of desperate defenders.

Crawling on her stomach, Cassandra crossed the verandah. Saul was being held under guard in the third room she tried.

'For the love of God!' she cried to the guards. 'Unshackle him! What chance would he stand, clapped in irons like this——'

Saul had been glancing out of a peephole in the door which looked out on to the verandah. 'Get back, Cassandra!' he shouted. 'Quickly—while the defence holds!'

'No,' she said quietly.

His face contorted. 'You fool! Don't make sacrifices for me! I don't want them. I don't want *you*. You mean nothing to me. *Get back while you still can!*'

Even as he spoke the Zulus began to swarm along the verandah, engaged in hand-to-hand fighting with the outnumbered soldiers.

There was no way out of the room except by the verandah. Again Cassandra demanded that Saul should be unshackled, and even the cautious guards agreed now that there was little likelihood of his escaping under the circumstances.

While they were removing the irons from Saul, Cassandra had become aware of a sound which was quite apart from the fighting going on along the verandah.

'Listen!' she cried. 'Someone is trying to hack through the wall. Someone else must be trapped in the next room!'

Very soon afterwards, first a crack formed in the interior wall between the rooms, and then a hole. A soldier appeared, dragging a patient with him, and went back for another. They heard a crash as the besieged door into the next room fell under the weight of Zulus.

'Oh God, they've got my mate!' the soldier shouted, kneeling by the hole and momentarily dropping his face in his hands. Saul pushed him aside, and lay on his stomach, groping for the tool with which the hole had been hacked in the wall.

It was a pickaxe. Swiftly and urgently, using his good arm, Saul began to hack away at the other internal wall, taking it in turns with the soldier whose pickaxe it was. The two guards defended the existing hole in the wall with their guns, holding off the Zulus who were trying to crawl through it into the room.

The other wall had now been breached, and they found themselves in a room with a rear door. The third room into which this opened contained eight more patients and a guard, but the original dilemma still remained. They were still trapped, with no way out save via the verandah. And the Zulus were relentlessly pressing in on them.

Someone offered Saul a rifle, but he refused it. 'I'll take my turn with the pickaxe,' he said shortly, 'and I'll drag the patients to safety. But I won't fire a gun at the Zulus.'

Once more the pickaxe was grimly applied, and once more they gained no more than a breathing space when a hole had been hacked in the wall. There was no way out of this room either; although it contained a door which led to the outside enclave, that door was besieged by the Zulus and there were no other exits into the main part of the building.

They dragged the patients through the hole, and set to work again with the pickaxe. Pausing to peer through a peephole, Cassandra noticed without realising its significance that burning assegais appeared to be raining on the building.

It was only several minutes later that the acrid odour reached her, and she understood.

'The building is on fire!' she gave the alarm. 'They've decided to burn us out!'

As the thatch blazed above their heads, the partition wall was attacked with desperation. The smoke was thick and choking, the roaring of the flames mingling with the crash of rifle-fire.

At last the new escape hole was big enough through which to drag the patients. Now they were in a long chamber, which had a window giving access to the enclave where the barriers still held. Inside this chamber were other patients, who were about to be evacuated by soldiers. Among the soldiers was Gwylfa Jones.

Cassandra hurried to speak to him. 'Bridget—is Bridget safe?'

'She is, Miss. She is with the patients who have already been evacuated to the stores compound.'

There was scarcely time to express relief. The timbers were burning now, lighting up the gathering darkness outside. They would have to brave the Zulus and cross the no-man's land towards the stores compound with the patients.

Each soldier and reasonably able-bodied patient was put in charge of one of the sicker or more disabled men.

Cassandra was allotted a young man with an injured leg.

One by one the patients slid or were pushed or man-handled through the window. Now they would have to be supported or humped as they ran the gauntlet of the Zulus, towards the compound. It was a slow, nerve-racking operation for they were forced to stop frequently and hold off the threatening waves of Zulus with their rifle-fire.

It was during one of these stops that Cassandra realised Saul was not among them. For the first time since this horror had engulfed her she lost control and became hysterical.

Sobbing, she abandoned her patient and turned back towards the burning building. A flying tackle from one of the soldiers brought her to the ground. Assegais whistled above their heads.

'Sorry, Miss,' the soldier apologised. 'Didn't mean to hurt you. But you can't go back there.'

'Saul Parnell is in there!' she screamed. 'Let go of me! I'm going to look for him!'

'No, Miss. It wouldn't be no use—Besides, he'll look after himself.'

'He's unarmed! How can he look after himself? *Let me go*!'

'It's too late, Miss,' the soldier said gently. 'You know it's too late. There ain't anything we could do for him now. You'd just be throwing your own life away too.'

CHAPTER
TEN

CASSANDRA had broken free of the soldier, and was beginning to run towards the hospital again, when she was caught from behind by Gwylfa Jones.

'Get you to the compound, Miss,' he said sternly. 'I shall go back for Parnell.'

'No!' She struggled wildly with him. 'I don't trust you! You've never done anything unless it was for yourself——'

'Maybe not. But I could never look Bridget in the face again if I let you go. And if *I* don't go, *you* will. So what I am about to do is not for you at all, do you see, nor indeed for Saul Parnell. It is for Bridget.'

He gave her a push in the direction of the others, and began to run in a zig-zag lope towards the burning building. Cassandra was forced to resume responsibility for her own charge, and continue on to the compound.

As soon as her patient had been delivered to the makeshift medical ward inside the compound, where Surgeon Major Reynolds was dressing and bandaging wounds, Cassandra ran outside again, straining her eyes against the smoke as she stared in the direction of the hospital building.

At last, silhouetted against the flames, she saw the figure of Gwylfa Jones humping a body on his back, running in a lurching motion to evade the Zulus.

Cassandra almost fainted with a reaction of mingled relief and horror when Jones finally reached the compound. Saul was alive, but badly hurt, with blood streaming from an assegai wound in his side. He was unconscious.

'I found him lying just inside the room, Miss,' Jones said. 'The assegai must have caught him as he was about to go through the window, and he fell backwards into the burning building.'

Saul was carried into the makeshift medical ward for the attention of Surgeon Major Reynolds, and Cassandra went to help Bridget with the tearing and rolling of bandages, desperately trying to keep her fears at bay.

By the light from the burning hospital building, the Zulus kept up their offensive. Gunfire crackled and assegais flew through the air as the night wore on, but the fighting became sporadic. The casualties on the Zulu side were heavy, and their morale was lowering.

Towards morning, the Zulu attacks petered out, and when dawn broke the only Zulus to be seen were the scores of dead which lay everywhere. A detail cleared a path through the bodies towards the cookhouse, to prepare breakfast. Miraculously, the British casualties consisted of only fifteen dead and twelve wounded.

After they had swallowed their breakfast, and before Cassandra could waylay Surgeon Major Reynolds for news of Saul, she and Bridget were summoned by a soldier for an interview with Lieutenant Bromhead. They found Gwylfa Jones in his presence, and Martin too.

'Well, young ladies,' Bromhead said briskly, 'I'm sending you and Mr Coleman back to D'Urban as soon as possible. For the sake of your own reputations, as well as for the sake of Army discipline, there will be no record that you were present during the battle.

'The record will merely show that you were found

wandering, having escaped from Zululand, and while you were trying to make your way to the Natal border.'

'I must own,' Martin said, 'that this is a considerable relief to me! I have been much concerned about my cousin's reputation——'

Bromhead gave him a steady look. It had not gone unnoticed that Martin had spent most of the battle locked in prayer inside the stores compound.

Then, ignoring the missionary, the officer glanced at Gwylfa Jones. 'As for you—Lieutenant Chard wishes your name to be included among those who are to be recommended for the Victoria Cross.'

'*Sir*?' Gwylfa Jones stared at him in blank amazement.

Lieutenant Bromhead permitted himself a slight, ironical smile. 'Your help in evacuating the patients from the burning hospital, as well as your courageous rescue of Saul Parnell, did not go unremarked. As there is nothing in the records to show that you do not deserve the V.C., I intend to endorse Lieutenant Chard's recommendation, subject to certain provisions which I will discuss with you later.'

'I beg your pardon, sir,' Jones said in a hard voice, 'but is this a joke of some kind? I have never heard of a V.C. being awarded to a——'

'To a soldier, Jones?' Bromhead interrupted swiftly. 'That is what you are. There are no records to show that you are otherwise.'

'But you were told, sir——'

'I am, unfortunately, hard of hearing, Private Jones. If—and I mean *if*—something was indeed said to me at some time, then I failed to catch it.'

He rose. 'You young ladies and Mr Coleman may go now. An escort will be ready later this morning to take you to D'Urban. Now, I wish to interview Infantryman Jones in private.'

Cassandra did not move. 'Lieutenant Bromhead Saul Parnell—?'

'Ah, yes.' Bromhead's voice was heavy and sombre now. 'I am afraid that the record is absolutely clear where *he* is concerned. He is wanted by the British Army to stand trial as a traitor and a spy.'

'He is neither! He showed stupendous courage in coming back to Rorke's Drift at the expense of his own safety, to warn of the Zulus' approach and to try and take us out of danger! Furthermore, Lieutenant, he did more than his share in rescuing the patients from the burning hospital——'

'I'm sorry, Miss Hudson. It is not in my power to do anything other than obey the regulations, and they state quite clearly that he must stand trial.'

'What—what will they do to him if he is found guilty?' Cassandra whispered. 'I mean—there were mitigating circumstances——'

Lieutenant Bromhead looked away. 'There could be only one outcome, I'm afraid. He will be hanged.'

The brutal word reverberated in Cassandra's ears. She stared at Lieutenant Bromhead. 'It's—obscene. Jones will get the Victoria Cross for saving his life, so that the British Army may take it instead ... *It's obscene!*'

Martin said repressively, 'Really, Cassandra, such excessive concern for a traitor doesn't become you——'

He was ignored. Lieutenant Bromhead came to Cassandra, and placed his arm about her shoulders 'I am extremely sorry, Miss Hudson. I can see how it must strike you, but those are the rules by which the Army functions. And if it's any comfort to you——' He stopped.

'Yes?' she urged, ready to grasp at any straw.

'If it's any comfort to you, Miss Hudson, Surgeon

Major Reynolds tells me that Saul Parnell is very gravely ill. It is highly unlikely that he will live to stand trial.'

Cassandra stared numbly at him. After a long while she whispered, through frozen lips, a plea to see Saul Lieutenant Bromhead nodded compassionately.

The memory of her last glimpse of Saul was to haunt her by day, and afford her no sleep at night. He was unconscious, with a wasted look about his face and an aura of death around him. And as if to underline the utter hopelessness of his position, an armed guard sat beside his bed in case he should recover and attempt to escape.

She touched his unaware face briefly with her lips, and stumbled out of the stores compound. Outside she found Gwylfa Jones waiting to say goodbye to her.

He gave her a sheepish smile. 'Perhaps I was wrong, Miss. All officers are not tarred with the same brush. Lieutenant Bromhead was tough on me after we were left alone together, but he is a man who sees further than his nose. I can respect him.'

Mechanically, Cassandra took his outstretched hand. 'I'm glad you've redeemed yourself, Jones. You were lucky to get a second chance.'

'And a share of the glory after all.' He nodded. 'There's ironical, isn't it, Miss. They are to pin a Victoria Cross on me, and the truth of it is that I only went to help with the evacuation of the patients because Bridget was inside the hospital.'

He could not have confirmed more clearly what Cassandra had suspected for some time—that he was in love with Bridget. As she made her way towards the wagon which was waiting to bear them to D'Urban, Cassandra felt weighed down by the sadness and futility of it all.

The journey back to D'Urban, escorted by two soldiers, became no more than a meaningless blur to her. She and Bridget shared the back of the wagon while Martin rode up front with the driver, which was a small blessing.

As if in an attempt to shift attention from his own less than noble conduct during the fighting, Martin took every opportunity of pointing out to Cassandra how shocking her behaviour had been from beginning to end. She sometimes wondered, with bitter humour, what he would say if he knew the full extent of what had happened to her since she travelled to Zululand and fell in love with Saul

Mechanically she answered when Bridget addressed her, and then fell once more into the tortured trap of her own thoughts. If she had never set out for Zululand, if she had never crossed the path of Cetewayo's white warrior, he would not now have been fighting for his life—a life which would speedily be taken by the British Army if he survived.

She could not escape the knowledge that she was indirectly to blame. If he had not had to concern himself with her affairs, he could have escaped from both the British and the Zulus immediately after he left Ulundi. And if he had not been weakened by his earlier wound and subsequent fever, he might have been better able to fight his present illness. And again she was to blame, for it had been she who shot him

In desperation, Cassandra tried to give her thoughts a different turn by concentrating on other matters. She looked at her plain little maid, whose aggressively red hair stood up in spikes about her face, and whose nose was now liberally sprinkled with freckles.

'You know, don't you, Bridget, that Gwylfa Jones is in love with you?'

'Oh, whisht, Miss Cassandra! What a thing to be

sayin'!' Bridget's face was suffused with colour.

'It's true, nevertheless. How do you feel about him?'

Bridget studied her hands. ''Tis not for me to be feelin' or not feelin', Miss Cassandra,' she burst out suddenly. 'Himself has said nothin' to me, and—and well, we've seen the way it is with the fightin', and men dyin' like flies . . . I'm sore afeared, Miss Cassandra, to feel *anything*, and that's the truth of it.'

Cassandra sighed. Yes, they had indeed seen the way it was. Nothing was certain, nothing at all. Who would have thought that the Zulus would devastate the mighty British at Isandhlwana? And who would have hazarded any money on the chances of a hundred men holding out against the massed ranks of Zulus at Rorke's Drift? Perhaps Bridget was wiser than her mistress, in not giving rein to her feelings while everything was so uncertain. There was an even chance that Gwylfa Jones would be killed during the war with the Zulus, now that he had been reinstated in the army.

Cassandra sighed again, more heavily. All in all, there could be very little future for Bridget and Jones. Even if he survived the war he would still remain a soldier, liable to be sent to whatever arena of war might arise in the future. He had no other means of earning his living, and how could he keep a wife on his Army pay?

Bridget broke into her thoughts. 'What will we do when we reach D'Urban, Mistress Cassandra? Will we take ship straightway for home?'

'No. We'll stay quietly at the Carlton until we know—until we know how the war is to end.'

But there was not to be any question of their staying quietly anywhere. News had travelled in advance, and all D'Urban it seemed had turned out to welcome their arrival in the port.

The whole of Natal had been convulsed with panic by the disaster of Isandhlwana; the Zulus had daily been

expected to sweep south over the border and follow up
their victory by demolishing the enemy on their home
ground.

In this atmosphere, the arrival of two girls who had
survived 'capture' by the Zulus was greeted with near
hysteria. They were acclaimed as heroines and accorded
a rapturous reception.

Among the dignitaries who met them were the
Reverend Pomfrey and his wife. They were old
acquaintances of Martin's, and insisted that he, and the
two girls, should stay with them in D'Urban.

'How—how kind,' Cassandra said with dismay, eyeing Mr and Mrs Pomfrey. The husband looked kindly
enough, but Mrs Pomfrey had the air of someone who
would be only too ready to condemn and pass judge
ment on lesser mortals

'However,' Cassandra continued, 'I shall not impose.
Bridget and I will go to the Carlton.'

'Nonsense,' Martin and Mrs Pomfrey said simultaneously. The latter went on, 'My dear Miss Hudson, I
always think there is something not quite *nice* about
even the most respectable hotels as far as unaccompanied young ladies are concerned.'

'I wouldn't be unaccompanied,' Cassandra pointed
out. 'I'd have Bridget with me——'

'Don't split hairs, Cassandra,' Martin said. 'We'll
accept my friends' kind invitation and stay at the vicarage, and that is the end of the matter.'

Cassandra flushed, and was about to make a mutin-
ous retort. But several correspondents of the world's
newspapers were among the crowd, and eager to question her and Bridget about their adventures, and they
closed in upon the two girls.

Afterwards they were borne away, willy-nilly, with
Martin and the Pomfreys. Soon after they had reached
the vicarage their hostess excused herself to supervise

the arrangements for lunch, while Bridget was taken off
to the servants' quarters. Mr Pomfrey had a sermon to
prepare in his study, so that Cassandra found herself
alone with Martin.

'Well, cousin,' he said, 'it seems that the world has
decided to see you as a celebrity and a heroine. You have
come better out of this escapade that I would have dared
to hope.'

'Yes, my reputation appears to be intact,' she agreed.
What a humbug he was!

He studied her, and said, 'I am sure you wish to
abandon that disreputable boys' garb and contrive a
more feminine coiffure, Cassandra, before you do anything else.'

She thrust her fingers through her short curls. 'There
is nothing I *can* do, save wait for it to grow again. And as
for my boys' clothing, it is all I have. I left my entire
wardrobe behind in Ulundi.'

'Mrs Pomfrey will, I am convinced, be more than
pleased to lend you some feminine garment,' Martin
insisted.

Cassandra thought of her hostess's tall, angular form.
'I shall look far more of a clown in Mrs Pomfrey's
clothes than I do at present,' she declared. 'You will just
have to resign yourself to seeing me like this, Martin,
for another few days yet.'

His mouth tightened. 'You show a regrettable vanity,
Cassandra. And I don't remember you as being so
wilful. You used to be more than happy to be guided by
me.' He placed his fingertips together in a pontificating
manner. 'I hope that being acclaimed a heroine has not
gone to your head. And while we are on the subject, I
still maintain that your proper course would have been
to remain in D'Urban until you heard from me.'

She thought of Saul, for whose desperate situation
she was entirely to blame, and said dully, 'I daresay you

are right.'

Martin smiled. 'Of course I am right! Had a fickle public not decided that your behaviour was heroic, an entirely different construction would have been placed on it, Cassandra. At the very least you would have been called a hoyden.'

She looked at her cousin, and said wearily, 'Do you think we might drop the subject now? You have lectured me quite enough.'

'There is one aspect on which I could not possibly lecture you enough, Cassandra,' Martin said heavily. 'I am referring to your strange and misguided friendship with Saul Parnell.'

'Don't criticise him!' Her voice was fierce. 'Don't say one word against him!'

'It almost seems as if the man has corrupted you, Cassandra——'

'*Corrupted!*' Her mouth began to tremble, so that she had to bite hard on her lip. 'If he has, then—then I am glad of it . . .'

Martin's face had darkened. 'Let me quote to you from the Scriptures, Cassandra. "*As a jewel of gold in a swine's throat, so is a fair woman who is without discretion!*"'

Cassandra rose, and moved towards the door. 'Have you always been so boring and absurd, Martin? If so, why had I never noticed?'

She did not give him time to react, but went in search of Mrs Pomfrey and begged to be allowed to retire to her room for the remainder of the day, pleading fatigue.

It was not, after all, a bad thing that Martin condemned her, and that they had quarrelled. The quotation which he had thrown at her must mean that he had read between the lines, and knew almost precisely what Saul had meant to her.

Very well, now she would be spared the necessity of

acting a part for Martin's benefit. How glad she was that
there had never been an engagement between them,
which would now have had to be broken. There had
been nothing between them, really, other than a misguided love on her part alone, and desire on his part to
improve her. Now he would feel that she was beyond
redemption by him.

Bridget came into her room to report that she had
been given accommodation in the servants' quarters,
and to ask if Cassandra required her for any duties.

Cassandra smiled wanly. 'Even if I had not decided to
dine in my room, Bridget, there would have been little
use in asking you to contrive a more feminine style for
my hair, which is what my cousin desired.'

Bridget gave her a sharp look. 'I'm thinkin', Miss
Cassandra, that yon spalpeen is not for you at all.'

'Spalpeen! That means a rascal, doesn't it? Martin is
depressingly pious and tedious, but he is hardly a
rascal.'

'No, Miss Cassandra? I have been keepin' me eyes
and ears open, and I'm thinkin' that Mr Martin has
grand plans for your money once he has married you!'

Cassandra shrugged, dismissing the matter. 'I am not
marrying my cousin, Bridget. We'll return to England
just as soon as I have had final news of——'

She could not bring herself to utter Saul's name, and
so she ended instead, 'of the war.'

But as the days passed it became clear to Cassandra
that there was more than a grain of truth in Bridget's
suspicions. For one thing, Martin had been suspiciously eager to patch up the quarrel between them.

'I have decided to forgive you, Cassandra,' he said
bombastically. 'You were not yourself, and I should
have borne that in mind. We'll say nothing more on the
subject. Your adventures in Zululand, too, shall remain
a closed book between us.'

That in itself was ominous. Martin would not have been prepared to sweep his suspicions about what had happened between her and Saul Parnell under the carpet unless he had a very strong motive for doing so.

Mrs Pomfrey too dropped veiled hints and uttered arch remarks which made it clear that she expected a marriage between Martin and his cousin. Cassandra tried to ignore them all, and concentrated her attentions on trying to gain news of Saul.

She followed reports of the continuing war with painful intensity, reading every line the newspapers printed in the fearful expectation of seeing a report of his death, either by natural causes or by execution. But there was never a clue to what had happened to him.

Great excitement reigned in D'Urban when Lord Chelmsford arrived from Zululand to give evidence at an official enquiry into the disaster at Isandhlwana. Using all her wiles and considerable cunning, Cassandra obtained an audience with him, but he could tell her little.

'Saul Parnell,' he said. 'Cetewayo's white warrior chief. . . . There has certainly been no trial as yet. The only report I have had on him was that he was lying dangerously ill in the hospital at Fort Helpmekaar. That was some while ago, so I daresay he has since died. His name would hardly have been included in any Roll of Honour.'

Cassandra would not, could not leave D'Urban until she was sure, beyond any doubt at all, that Saul *was* dead. She wrote a letter to the officer in command of Helpmekaar, requesting news of Saul or of Gwylfa Jones. The latter might know more than the authorities were willing to disclose.

But no reply came, and in the meantime Martin was making it abundantly clear that he expected to marry Cassandra, that he had always expected it and that it was more or less her duty to fall in with his wishes.

Cassandra often yearned to know who the married woman was in D'Urban, who had Saul's love. She would have liked to make her acquaintance and talk to her of him. It would have been painful, but she longed for any kind of link with him, however tenuous. And the woman might have news of him. *Any* kind of news would have been more bearable than this endless waiting.

One morning Martin said, with deceptive casualness, 'I really do feel it is time we named the day, Cassandra. Now that the war is drawing to a close and the heathen Zulus have been suitably chastened, the Lord's work calls. There is much to be done.'

'Are you,' Cassandra demanded, 'proposing to me Martin?'

He shrugged. 'A proposal is not really necessary. It was always understood between us.'

'It was not understood by *me*——' she began.

'Come now, Cassandra! Why else did you travel all the way from England? Why else did you brave the hazards of Zululand against all advice?'

There was no convincing answer to that, and his smug expression told Cassandra that he was well aware of it. 'You've never even kissed me,' she said at a tangent, 'except on the forehead.'

'Certainly not!' he agreed austerely. 'I have always deplored vulgar and ostentatious expressions of feeling. There is far more between us than kisses and caresses, my dear.'

'What, exactly, *is* there between us, Martin?' she asked. 'As far as I can tell, you disapprove of me utterly, if you find me attractive, you certainly don't show it I should have thought that from your point of view, I would make the most unsuitable missionary's wife. Is it, perhaps, that the important thing between us, the *only* thing, is my money?

He flushed, but he did not avoid her eyes. 'You put it very crudely, Cassandra. But you did indicate in your letters to me that you wished to place your inheritance at my disposal, and indeed I can think of no more suitable purpose to which it could be put. Your money would amply endow a mission school in Zululand. Think of it, Cassandra—The Martin Coleman School for Zulu Converts!'

She did think of it She also thought of Saul, and for the first time she shared his general opinion of missionaries. Martin's ambitions had very little to do with a genuine desire to help the Zulus He wanted to immortalise his name and gain a little corner of history for himself.

She rose 'I'm sorry, Martin. I am not going to marry you, or endow your Mission School'

The atmosphere in the household became very strained after that. Martin had too much dignity to plead with Cassandra, but he made it plain that she was being unbelievably selfish and wrong-minded, and it was obvious that Mrs Pomfrey agreed with him. Cassandra would have liked to move to the Carlton while she awaited the end of the war, and definite news at last of Saul. But when she suggested it Mrs Pomfrey became so affronted that Cassandra dropped the subject and allowed the situation to remain in abeyance.

Then came the morning when Bridget arrived in Cassandra's bedroom, her cheeks flushed. She did not look at Cassandra as she held out a letter to her.

'It came for me this morning, Miss Cassandra. It's from—from Gwylfa Jones Please read it.

Her heart pounding sickeningly in her breast, Cassandra smoothed out the pages. Bridget would not have offered it to her to read unless it contained news of Saul.

But the long letter seemed to be little more than a detailed account of the war. From Rorke's Drift, Gwylfa Jones had been sent to Eshowe, where he had taken part in the siege. The Zulus had sustained appalling losses, he reported. Some time after that, he had been with Chelmsford's army advancing on Ulundi.

'I could not help but put myself in the place of the Zulus,' Jones had written. 'I knew so well how the scene must have struck them, watching from the Royal *kraal*.

'The army advanced in one vast hollow square, all the bands playing, the regimental colours flying. The Imperial infantry marched in sections of four, and in the walls of the rectangle were the Ninetieth Foot, the Cameronians, and the Ninety-fourth; the Thirteenth Foot, the Somerset Light Infantry, the Fifty-eighth, the South Staffordshires. Inside the square were the general's staff, the ammunition carriages and the native troops, together with the Seventeeth Lancers and the Dragoon Guards.

'Do you remember that day when Cetewayo's impis sought to impress us with their military might and pageantry at Ulundi, Bridget? I wonder what they thought as they watched us marching in all our glory upon them.

'Do you not think they would have been awed by those ranks of scarlet infantry, by the pennons of the Lancers in their blue uniforms, by the great standards inscribed in gold, by the sun glinting on all those bayonets and on the cannon brass? Do you not think they would have been impressed by the blaring of the musical instruments as the band played a military march?

'We shall never know what their reactions were at the sight, for over a thousand of them are dead, and the survivors scattered. They gave us a good run for our money, mind.

'They had very little left to lose, of course. Their home villages had been burnt down during the war, their kith and kin slaughtered, their *kraals* pillaged and their oxen driven away. And now Ulundi, their pride, their Royal *kraal*, was about to be razed to the ground. Foolish dignity would not allow them to surrender and watch the destruction of Ulundi, and so they came at us. It was national suicide. Young boys and old men came at us, to pit their assegais against our Gatling guns. Afterwards we set fire to all the huts in Ulundi.

'I almost forgot to mention that the British sustained the loss of only ten men killed. Was not that a great triumph for the Army, a battle that will remain alive in the history books?

'The war is all but over, Bridget. Cetewayo and his family escaped from Ulundi before the British marched on the Royal *kraal*, and the task now only remains to find him before the Zulu nation can be said to be effectively destroyed for ever.'

Cassandra paused in the reading of the letter. She could well imagine Gwylfa Jones's searing bitterness as he penned his account. He had not really changed his opinions on war after all. . . .

She returned to the letter. 'I am buying myself out of the army, Bridget. And now comes my principal reason for writing to you. I obtained your address from Lieutenant Bromhead. I am asking you to marry me, *cariad*. And before you think I have nothing to offer you, let me put you straight.

'Just before he died, Saul Parnell made me a gift of his farm in Ireland . . .'

CHAPTER
ELEVEN

THE writing blurred before Cassandra's eyes. She laid the letter down and gave Bridget a blind, stricken look.

'Oh, my dear Mistress Cassandra!' the maid whispered, and began to weep softly.

Cassandra's anguish went too deep for tears. A cold, logical part of her mind was reasoning, *Why are you so shocked, so shattered? You must have known in your heart that he was dead. For if he hadn't been, he would have been put on trial, and there would have been so much publicity that news could not have failed to reach you.*

Mechanically, she picked up the letter again and forced herself to re-read that dreadful sentence.

'Just before he died, Saul Parnell made me a gift of his farm in Ireland. How it came about was like this——

'Before going to Eshowe, I was stationed for a brief while at Fort Helpmekaar, and whilst there Saul Parnell was also there in the hospital, fighting for his life. He rallied for a while and learnt that I had dragged him out of the burning hospital at Rorke's Drift. I was given permission to visit him several times and we grew to understand one another well.

'Then he had a relapse, and even he knew that he was dying. He wished to put his affairs in order before the end.

'It seems that he owned large estates in Ireland, Bridget. He has willed it all to Miss Hudson, with the exception of the home farm. He wished me to have that. In order that I should not have to involve myself in legal complexities, he made me an outright gift of the farm. It was all done properly, with witnesses and whatever, so the property has been mine from that day, and I have been drawing revenue from it. I know I can make a go of the farm, *cariad*, if you would marry me.'

I can't bear it, something inside Cassandra screamed with violent rebellion. *It's not fair . . .*

She thrust the letter aside and began to walk aimlessly about the room, her arms hugging her breast as if her pain were physical. She could see her future stretching before her, empty and meaningless, with no comfort anywhere.

Bridget's hesitant voice broke through her despair. 'He must have—loved you very much, Mistress Cassandra, or he would not have left you everything in his will.'

She turned her unseeing gaze on Bridget, and slowly the meaning of Saul's will began to seep through the chaos and anguish of her mind.

The married woman in D'Urban did not matter, if she had ever existed at all. Only now that it was too late, Cassandra could see why he had seemed to reject her love. He had known that he was doomed, and had wanted to spare her. But he *had* loved her. From that knowledge she would gain comfort of a kind. It was all she was to have.

Cassandra spoke for the first time since Bridget had given her the letter to read. Her voice sounded dry and rusty.

'You'll marry Gwylfa Jones, of course.'

'Oh no, Mistress! I'm not after leavin' you!'

But Cassandra knew that that was where her heart really lay. 'You can't sacrifice your own happiness for me, Bridget. I won't let you. You must write to Mr Jones, and tell him that you will marry him when he has gained his discharge from the Army.'

Bridget's face settled into stubborn lines. But a thought occurred to her, and a gleam of excitement entered her eyes. 'I'll do as you say, Mistress Cassandra, on one condition! If you will make your home on Mr Parnell's Irish estate, so that I may go on servin' you!'

'Why not?' Cassandra returned recklessly. What did it matter where she lived from now on? 'I dare say I shall hear from the Irish lawyers in due course. These things take time.' She looked away. 'Please don't mention this legacy in my cousin's hearing.'

Martin would mutter bitterly on the injustice of a fate which heaped more and more riches on someone who was already an heiress, while he could not afford to endow his mission school for Zulu converts. He would hint that, since Cassandra would not consent to marry him, she should at least share her wealth with him.

Indeed, if she could have been certain that the money really would benefit the Zulus, and not foster Martin's ambitions and self-aggrandisement, there was nothing she would have liked better than to turn the revenue from her legacy over to him. It would have been a fitting memorial to Saul. If only Martin could have been trusted . . .

The thought remained in her mind as the days passed, empty of any comfort or hope, and she tried to dull her pain by concentrating on ways and means of creating some kind of memorial to Saul.

He had loved the Zulu nation; they had been his adopted people. And now they were scattered and broken, no longer a nation. There had to be some way in which she could help them in his name.

A mission or school of some kind was the obvious answer, somewhere where children could learn to read and write, not only English but also their own language.

A place where they could be inspired with a pride in their own culture, but also taught to adapt themselves to a modern and changing world.

She could not trust anyone else to carry out her wishes faithfully. Whichever missionary she appointed as her agent would inevitably impose his own ideas and principles on the school. And unless she became a missionary herself the authorities would not allow her to enter Zululand and establish her school. But apart from the fact that she had no vocation for it, becoming a missionary would take too long . . .

Gradually, it came to Cassandra that the logical solution was to marry Martin after all. As his wife, she could return to Magwana and build the mission school *her* way, manage it as *she* wished to, in accordance with what Saul would have wanted. The Saul Parnell Memorial School for Zulu Children . . .

What did it matter that she no longer even liked Martin, let alone loved him? There was no one else she would ever wish to marry, now that Saul was dead. As Martin's wife, she would at least have some purpose in life, something to work for.

Once she had reached her decision, Cassandra lost no time in telling Martin that she had changed her mind. She had no feeling of guilt at all, no sense of cheating him out of anything.

His reaction was almost too smug to be borne. 'I'm glad you've come to your senses, Cassandra! I'll have the banns put up immediately, so that we may be married with the greatest possible speed. In the meantime I shall have plans drawn up for the building of a mission school. I know just what I want.'

No, there was no need whatever to feel guilty because she was using Martin. He would not have dreamt of marrying her if she had been penniless. He did not really want a wife at all; he was a cold, undemonstrative man. All he wanted was her money.

She said mildly, 'Don't you think I might like to be consulted about the plans for the mission school, since I shall be paying for it?'

He gave her a condescending smile. 'My dear Cassandra, practical matters like those are my province. I shall bear all the responsibilities and take all the decisions once we are married, and of course the law will give me complete control of your money. That is entirely as it should be.'

Cassandra said nothing. What Martin obviously did not know was that, in response to continued agitation by the British public, that particular iniquitous law was about to be changed. By the time it came to paying for the mission school, Martin would discover that a married woman's property was no longer legally her husband's. She would allow him to dream his complacent dreams until then.

In the meantime, the household was plunged into feverish preparations for the wedding. Mr Pomfrey had offered to give Cassandra away, and the reception was to be held at the vicarage. To everyone's disapproval Cassandra insisted that Bridget should be her bridesmaid. Apart from this one particular issue, Cassandra felt detached from all the arrangements, as if she were not involved in them at all.

It was only when Bridget had helped her into her wedding gown, and she stared at her reflection in the mirror, that the stark realisation washed into Cassandra's brain *In an hour's time I shall be irrevocably Martin's wife.*

Even if she had wished to, she could not stop it now. Already Martin had left for the church, and the bridal carriage was waiting outside for Cassandra and Bridget and Mr Pomfrey. It was too late to change her mind, or alter her fate

She closed her eyes, shutting out the reflection of herself in her bridal gown, and for a brief moment allowed raw pain and despair to wash over her. Then she turned away, and squared her shoulders.

'Let us go, Bridget.'

Outside in the hall, Mr Pomfrey stepped forward to offer her his arm. And then they were inside the carriage, and Cassandra stared unseeingly through the window as the decorated horses began to high-step along D'Urban's dusty street towards the church.

To the amazed disbelief of the medical officers, Saul Parnell had clung to life long after all hope had been abandoned for him. His affairs had been put in order, the home farm in Ireland assigned to Gwylfa Jones, his will leaving everything else to Cassandra witnessed and signed.

Because of his Irish name, and because it was assumed that he had been baptised into the Catholic church, a priest performed the last rites, and still Saul refused to abandon his slender hold on life.

Gwylfa Jones had long since left Helpmekaar for Eshowe, not doubting for a moment that Saul had died as everyone expected him to. But, defying all medical opinion, the sick man fought on.

He was not aware that he was fighting for his life. He dwelled in a strange limbo in which his own hallucinations became intermingled with reality, and he imagined that he was being kept a prisoner, tied down and helpless. The medical staff were all enemies who were keeping him there, preventing him from reaching Cassandra, who was facing some unknown danger. He had to outwit them somehow; he had to escape and go to Cassandra's aid.

In an ironical way his long battle for life was saving him from another fate. While it lasted he could not be tried for treason, and with each week that passed, each month, the issue became more blurred at the edges as the war altered circumstances.

After the appalling losses suffered by the Zulus at Eshowe, British rockets and shells tore fearsome gaps in the impis at Gingindhlovu. Anyone would have thought that after the burning of Ulundi, the destruction of the Royal *kraal* and the slaughter of some seven thousand warriors the spirit of the Zulus would have been broken.

But hopelessly outmatched and outclassed as they were, small pockets of resistance continued to meet the British forces, and Cetewayo himself still eluded them. Until the King had been captured his people would not admit defeat. Finding Cetewayo became the Army's most urgent priority.

British search parties came up against a stone wall. No matter what threats they uttered, or how much they offered in bribes, not one Zulu would give so much as a clue as to where the King might be hiding. Even when the British searchers, in frustration and desperation, resorted to physical intimidation, the Zulus remained steadfastly loyal to their King.

This was the situation when, after months in the hospital at Helpmekaar, Saul Parnell was finally judged fit to stand trial. But the officers there, aware of the abortive and now desperate search for Cetewayo, had perceived a way in which Parnell could be of more use to them alive than dead.

Saul had recovered to the extent where it was considered necessary to have two armed guards at his side at all times. One morning an officer, Lieutenant-Colonel Darcey, arrived at Helpmekaar to see him.

'If you would lead us to the Zulu King,' he said, 'we would drop all charges against you. You must know all the hiding places which Cetewayo could conceivably use.'

'No,' Parnell said quietly.

'We're offering you your life, and your freedom!'

'The price is too high.'

The officer attempted to hide his frustration. 'Think about it. I'll give you time to change your mind.'

Saul's grim smile indicated that there was no likelihood of his changing his mind. 'While you're waiting to persuade me,' he suggested, 'may I have writing materials? I wish to send a letter to someone.'

'No. I'm sorry. The Army is understandably anxious not to have it known that we are attempting to bargain with you for your life. You will not be allowed to communicate with anyone unless and until you have accomplished what we wish you to do.'

The officer went away, and Saul racked his brains for ways and means of sending one last message to Cassandra. But his guards were completely incorruptible and they made certain that he did not have contact with anyone who might have been prepared to smuggle a message out for him.

Lieutenant-Colonel Darcey returned again and again to argue with him, or to appeal to his sense of self-preservation.

'You would not be betraying Cetewayo if you led us to him,' he urged. 'We do not seek to take his life, we only wish to banish him into exile.'

'*Only*?' Saul returned with bitter irony. 'You wish to remove the lynch-pin which holds the Zulu nation together, and you expect my help!'

'Heavens, man, think of your own skin, if nothing else! Do this one thing for us, and you'll be free!'

But when Saul did capitulate in the end it was not the thought of his own survival which motivated him. Even held in isolation within the hospital as he was, accounts of the desultory battles still being waged percolated through to him, and he began to perceive that while Cetewayo remained free his impis would never give in. The slaughter on both sides would go needlessly on. He would have to betray the King so that the killing could stop.

A triumphant Lieutenant-Colonel Darcey sent Saul Parnell from Fort Helpmekaar with a contingent of soldiers. The soldiers were not only there to deal with any resistance from King Cetewayo's bodyguards; they were also Saul's custodians, ensuring that he fulfilled his obligations and did not escape. Only when King Cetewayo had been found would Saul be free to go his own way.

Several weeks later Saul tracked the King down. With a pathetic little party of his wives and children, he had taken refuge in a *kraal* in the Ngoma forest. There was no attempt at resistance as the British entered the *kraal*.

Ignoring the soldiers, Saul went to kneel in homage before the King. 'Majesty,' he said with despair, 'why in God's name did you let it come to this?'

'I tried, my son,' Cetewayo replied wearily. 'I did not wish for war in the first place. You know that. And when it came I sent envoy after envoy to the British, asking for peace talks. My messengers were abused or ignored or taken prisoner.'

He dropped his head in his hands. 'An assegai has been plunged into the side of my nation, and there are not tears enough in the world to mourn the dead.'

'Majesty——' Saul touched his shoulder. 'I have to ask you to surrender yourself to the soldiers, so that the killing may stop.'

When Cetewayo lifted his face, tears glistened on his cheeks. 'If you love me, my son,' he pleaded, 'then do something for me. Take my hunting spear and thrust it through my heart, so that I may die with my nation.'

'The nation will rise again——'

'No. What the mighty Chaka created has been destroyed for ever. And I shall be as a dead man too from now on.'

Cetewayo rose. Like an old and beaten man he moved towards the soldiers, begging them to kill him. Saul gestured to the soldiers that he intended to stay at the *kraal* for a while, and turned his back so that he would not have to see the King being borne away, a prisoner.

After he had given such comfort as he could to Cetewayo's wives and children, Saul left to begin the long journey out of Zululand. South of Pietermaritzburg he caught up with Gwylfa Jones's regiment, and immediately went in search of the Welshman.

Jones's first reaction of incredulity and pleasure became tempered with wary self-interest.

'You'll be wanting your farm back, isn't it,' he said flatly.

Saul laughed. 'No, don't worry. In fact, I'll be glad to have you on the home farm. You could advise me on the running of the estate. I know nothing of such matters. I'm planning to marry Miss Hudson, you see, and live in Ireland with her——'

A Welsh oath from Gwylfa Jones interrupted him. 'It's sorry I am, *bach*, to be telling you this! Miss Hudson is to marry her cousin the day after tomorrow. I am engaged to Bridget, do you see, and she wrote to give me the news——'

Saul was no longer listening. A fierce look had entered his eyes. 'I have to stop them.'

'You'll not get there in time.'

'I will. I must.' Even as he spoke Saul had turned away, and was hurrying to saddle his stallion once more. Pausing only to ask for Cassandra's address, he streaked from the camp with a wild clatter of hoofs.

Logic and common sense told him that Jones was right; he could not cover the distance to D'Urban in time. But something inside him refused to listen to logic or common sense as he set both himself and his stallion a punishing course. He saw none of the beauty of the Valley-of-a-Thousand-Hills through which he travelled; he was unconscious of the heat and the dust, and he bitterly resented the stops he was forced to make for his horse's sake.

As he rode into D'Urban on Cassandra's wedding day he could hear the church bells tolling. Grimly, he urged his stallion on. At the far end of the long, dusty street he could see the bridal carriage waiting, its horses decorated with ribbons, flowers and ostrich feathers. He narrowed his eyes against the sun's glare and the dust. Now he could see figures moving towards the carriage, Cassandra recognisable by the white blur of her wedding gown.

He tried to spur his stallion into greater effort, but he had finally asked to much of the poor beast. The stallion stumbled, its front legs buckling beneath the weight they were carrying. The animal could go no further.

Saul shouted to a street urchin to look after him, and then he cupped his hands to his mouth, shouting Cassandra's name. His voice was borne mockingly back to him on the breeze.

The carriage moved away. Finding reserves of strength from somewhere, Saul sprinted after it, thrusting pedestrians out of the way, his strained, intent gaze keeping the carriage in sight.

Just when he thought that he, too, would topple over through sheer exhaustion like his stallion, a hackney cab came clopping down the road. Saul heaved himself aboard, and gasped, 'Driver—overtake that carriage in front—and there's a sovereign in it for you.'

The driver needed no further urging. They were

gaining on the bridal carriage when, just ahead of them, the door of one of D'Urban's saloons burst open and a crowd surged out, spilling into the street. A fight had broken out, and as the mob spurred the combatants on all traffic was forced to come to a halt. By the time the street was cleared once more, the bridal carriage had disappeared from view. Saul urged the driver on grimly. He had not come this far to admit defeat now.

When they saw the carriage again it was empty, standing outside a church. Saul sprang from the cab and shouted to the driver to wait. Then he was speeding to the door of the church.

Heads turned as he entered, and a muted gasp went up from the congregation. They craned their necks to watch the tall, dishevelled man in his dusty clothes stride unceremoniously up the aisle. His grin of relief when he realised that the wedding service had not yet reached the point of no return gave him a satanic look, coupled as it was with his brilliant blue gaze and his days'-old stubble of beard.

Cassandra was so deeply locked in apathy and numb acceptance that she was unaware of the intrusion. She stood with bowed head, waiting fatalistically for the ceremony to take its course and tie her to Martin.

'*Holy Mother of God!*' She heard Bridget's shocked gasp behind her, and turned her head.

It was too much, she thought confusedly. Why must Saul's ghost haunt her on this of all occasions?

'Cassandra,' he said softly, making a question of her name, ignoring Martin's expression of outrage and the vicar's perplexed frown.

Everything began to spin around her. Saul elbowed Martin out of his way and caught her in his arms as she fainted.

A kind of restrained, respectful pandemonium broke out in the church. People stood up in their seats or milled forward, eager not to miss any of this extraordinary drama. The vicar kept his head, and ordered Cassandra to be carried into the vestry.

She opened her eyes. Saul's face—dusty, unshaven and haggard, but unmistakably his face—swam before her gaze. Could it be a cruel hoax, a mirage, an hallucination? She lifted a hand, and touched the reassuringly real stubble on his cheek.

'I thought—you were dead . . .'

'We all thought you were dead,' Martin's voice interrupted, cold with contained anger. 'What right do you think you have to barge in and turn our wedding into a spectacle?'

'I have something pressing to say to Cassandra.' Saul turned to the vicar. 'I'm sorry about the timing. Do you think we could have a few minutes' privacy?'

For the first time Cassandra became aware that the Pomfreys and some of their friends had crowded into the vestry too. At the vicar's insistence the onlookers began to melt away.

Martin said angrily, 'This is outrageous! I insist on remaining——'

But the vicar took his arm, and steered him gently towards the door. When it closed behind them Saul drew Cassandra to her feet and stood looking at her, without attempting to touch her. She gazed back at him.

There were unfamiliar hollows in his cheeks, and his mouth had a grimness which had not been there before. But his intensely blue eyes held a look of tenderness and longing as they gazed down at her.

'Well, Cassandra,' he said softly, 'do you want to go ahead and marry your saintly cousin?'

'My saintly——' Her voice caught. 'Oh, Saul, I only agreed to marry him because I was sure you were dead. Why did Gwylfa Jones lie?'

'He didn't lie.' Swiftly, Saul told her what had happened.

She covered her face with her hands. 'It's too late, Saul. I've gone too far to turn back.'

'It's not too late,' he said roughly. 'All you have to do is to go out there and announce that you've made a mistake, and that you've changed your mind.'

'I can't do it——'

He pulled her close and took her lips in a kiss that was savage in its intensity. 'You told me once that you loved me,' he said, lifting his head. 'I remember every single thing about that moment—how you looked, with the bright sun on your absurd boyish curls, the way your eyes changed colour as you spoke, the way I felt. Especially the way I felt. Do you think I would let you go, just because you don't have the courage to face all those people out there?'

'It—isn't for want of courage,' she said unsteadily. 'Saul, how could I do such a thing to Martin? Even knowing that he doesn't love me? How could I humiliate him in such a public and sensational way? He would never live it down——'

'Miss Hudson is right,' the vicar's voice said from the doorway. Neither of them had been conscious of the fact that he had returned to the vestry. He looked at them, his eyes wise and kind and full of understanding.

'It would be a terrible thing to do to any man,' he went on.

Saul bit off an oath. 'So she is to marry him, knowing that she is making a mistake, that she will be wretched——'

'No.' The vicar smiled faintly. 'But Martin's face must be saved. What I propose is this. Help Miss Hudson through the vestry window, and make yourselves scarce. I shall return to the congregation and announce that the bride is unwell, and that the wedding will have to be postponed. The truth will come out later, of course, but Martin will be able to keep his dignity. Go now, quickly.'

A short while later Cassandra, breathless and with her wedding veil tangled and awry, was speeding towards the waiting cab, Saul's hand firmly on her arm. The church choir, she noted dazedly, was singing a rousing hymn. Nothing seemed real.

Reality returned sharply when the cab began to sway along the street. She looked at Saul with helpless dismay. 'I can't go back to the Pomfreys'! Even if they would have me under their roof again, I couldn't——'

'No,' he agreed calmly. 'Our behaviour has already been so outrageous that there is little point in holding on to what remains of our reputation. We're going to the Carlton, where I have a suite permanently reserved.'

Their arrival at the hotel caused a minor sensation, but they were oblivious of it, and quite unaware of the incongruous sight they presented, with Cassandra in her bridal finery and Saul dusty and dishevelled.

When they gained his suite he pulled her into his arms, and kicked the door shut behind them.

His mouth moved along the side of her face, touching her cheek. 'I'm afraid this is going to mean a permanent breach with Martin, your only living relative,' he murmured.

'I know. Poor Martin, he had his heart set on my inheritance . . .'

Then Saul's hands moved along the curve of her body, and she dismissed all thoughts of Martin. Her head was forced back by his mouth on her own.

The unconscious memory of past rebuffs caused her to hold back, afraid of betraying herself too nakedly. He fumbled for her hands and slid them against his chest, so that she could feel the uneven vibration of his heart under her fingers. His lips became hungry and demanding on hers, and this time she responded with all the passion of longing and heartbreak which had tormented her for so long.

When he lifted his head there was both tenderness and desire in his eyes as he looked down at her; and Cassandra could only marvel that a day which had started with such doom and hopelessness could have ended this way.

Don't miss these exciting Masquerades!

57. Captain Black by Caroline Martin

A sober and dutiful young woman of strict Puritan upbringing finds her life changed forever by a single incredible encounter on a lonely darkened road..

58. Meeting at Scutari by Belinda Grey

An impossible love, a yearning for something more than the boring existence of the idle rich in Victorian England, takes the impetuous Jessica Linton on a journey that changes her life forever....

59. The Devil's Angel by Ann Edgeworth

A beautiful young woman, fresh into the fashionable society of 1770 London, tries desperately to fight her attraction for a handsome duke–for he wants a mistress, not a wife!

60. Cromwell's Captain by Anne Madden

A moving tale of a love seemingly doomed before it starts. A pretty Royalist girl falls prey to the charms of a handsome wounded soldier–a captain in Cromwell's army!

61. House of Satan by Gina Veronese

When Eloise meets her new guardian, she discovers not the elderly roué she had been led to expect, but a handsome young count with a deep and sorrowful secret. Set in Vienna, 1785.

62. Tarrisbroke Hall by Jasmine Cresswell

An impoverished earl reluctantly realizes he must marry into a plebeian fortune. His bride-to-be is expected to be delighted at the match; instead her reaction is utter, helpless fury!

Masquerade
Romantic Novels of Long Ago

Masquerade romances are books
of love and adventure, suspense and intrigue,
set in times long past. Beautiful novels
that will sweep you away... to the colorful
world of Regency London... to the searing
passions of Czarist Russia... to the
tumultuous shores of Revolutionary France.

•

Many previously published titles are once
again available.
Choose from this exciting collection!

Masquerade
historical romances

Choose from this list of early titles.

Relive a great love story...
Masquerade romances